MIDNIGHT
WEDDING

MIDNIGHT WEDDING

BY

SOPHIE WESTON

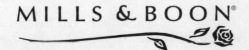

MILLS & BOON®

First published in Great Britain 2000 Large Print edition 2001 Harlequin Mills & Boon Limited, Eton House, 18-24 Paradise Road, Richmond, Surrey TW9 1SR

© Sophie Weston 2000

ISBN 0 263 16779 8

Set in Times Roman 15½ on 17 pt. 16-0601-55513

Printed and bound in Great Britain by Antony Rowe Ltd, Chippenham, Wiltshire

PROLOGUE

THE group of international journalists was miserable. Ignaz was fourteen thousand feet up in the Andes. The near-vertical track had challenged even the state-of-the-art Land Rover. The rain was relentless, the disaster site was a uniform mud colour and the press officer was clearly out of his depth.

'What the hell am I going to photograph?' muttered *Elegance* magazine's star feature writer.

'It will stop in half an hour,' said a crisp voice behind them.

They all swung round. And saw a Greek god in khaki shorts. There was a silence filled with something between awe and screaming resentment.

'Jack,' said the press officer with unmistakable relief. 'Ladies and gentlemen, this is Dr Jack Armour.'

'Oh, wow,' said *Elegance* magazine reverentially.

It was not difficult to see why. Dr Jack Armour was tall. Not just tall, but somehow larger than life. His skin was tanned to dark gold and you could see a lot of it. In contrast to the journalists huddling in their protective clothing, he wore the minimum, magnificently impervious to the steady downpour. Droplets ran down the muscled chest, darkening the dusting of hair there to black. His long legs were bare.

'Dr Armour is the American expert I was telling you about. It is he who will show you round the emergency recovery site. Please feel free to ask him anything you want.'

'Dr Armour!' muttered *Elegance* magazine. 'That is sex on a stick.' She raised her camera.

'Good morning,' said the Greek god, amused.

He led the way up the hillside, moving as easily as a mountain goat, while he kept up a level of informed commentary. The muscular legs made nonsense of the mud, the slope and the ice-rink-slippery patches of exposed rock. Rain dripped off him. He seemed unaware of it, even though his sleeveless cotton jacket left his arms and much of his bronzed chest naked to the elements.

The journalists breathed hard.

'Sorry about the pace,' he said over his shoulder. 'I've got to wind this up fast. I'm flying to Paris today.'

'Lucky you,' said one of the panting journalists ruefully.

'I hate the place. But there's a meeting I can't miss.'

Elegance magazine was shocked and said so. 'Hate Paris? City of culture, city of lovers?'

Jack Armour laughed aloud at that. 'When I go to Paris I'll be concentrating on natural disaster statistics. No sight-seeing. No sex.'

She pursed her red-painted mouth. 'So when do you do your—sight-seeing?' The last two words were loaded with meaning.

The laughter died out of his face, leaving his eyes so dark they looked black in the sulphurous light.

'Shut up,' hissed a British journalist out of the corner of his mouth. He knew the man and his sore points.

Jack Armour ignored him and fixed *Elegance* magazine with a level gaze. It made her shift uncomfortably, a new experience for her.

'A guy in my line of work has no time for— sight-seeing,' he said deliberately.

'But—'

'*Shut up,*' the British journalist hissed again.

Jack's expression was as yielding as steel. 'Tried it. Found it doesn't work. End of experiment.'

Something in the harsh voice silenced even *Elegance* magazine.

CHAPTER ONE

HOLLY stepped carefully out of the elevator, balancing her tower of caterer's boxes with concentration. She was working hard to repress a superstitious shiver. She hated these huge, impersonal buildings, no matter how luxurious. They reminded her of visiting her mother at work in that vast office in London.

Most of the time she managed to forget all of that: mother, London and that other life. It was nearly eight years ago, after all. Then a train crash had taken her mother's life and, along with it, every familiar thing in Holly's schoolgirl existence. It sometimes seemed to her that ever since, wherever she was, she had been a stranger passing through.

The mirrored doors of the elevator reflected back just how much of a stranger. These days she hardly recognised herself. She had shot up on long colt's legs. Her mid-brown hair had lightened. Now in some lights it almost looked gold. It was still uncontrollably curly. So she kept it long and plaited it for work. Now in her dungarees and baseball cap she looked like a gawky schoolboy.

Here in Paris she had been reborn as a delivery boy, she thought wryly. For the time being.

Her mother, she now realised, had tried to prepare her for life's unpredictability.

'Everything's temporary, Hol,' she would say, over and over.

All these years later, Holly could recall her huge eyes. Even when she was laughing with her daughter they had always seemed sad.

'You've got to look after yourself,' she would mutter, hugging Holly to her suffocatingly. 'Nobody else will.' And then, when she was exhausted, beyond laughter or sadness, 'Forgive me.'

Of course Holly had not known there was anything to forgive then. Or nothing more than half her class had to forgive, chiefly the frequent absence of an overworked career mother. She had never known her father. She could not guess that her mother had left a message for him in her will.

But she had. A shocked and grieving Holly had found herself tidied up and transferred to his millionaire's home in the American mid-West before she knew what was happening to her. So that was when she had discovered for herself the other great truth her mother had bequeathed her: 'You can't trust a man, except to break your heart.'

Holly gave herself a mental shake. That was all behind her now. Well behind her. The father she had never really known was dead. The stepsister who had been affronted by her very existence was far away; five years and a whole continent away.

And if that meant that Holly was alone—well, fine. If her heart was lost in ice floes at least no one could get at it. She was footloose and solitary and *safe*.

Congratulating herself on her successful life planning, she hefted the boxes into a more comfortable position and started to plod off along the miles of deep-piled silence to the offices of the International Disaster Committee.

'Thank you, gentlemen,' said the Chair. 'You have given us a lot to think about.' It was dismissal.

Jack bit back a protest. He had not yet covered half the topics he had prepared. There should have been plenty of time. He had established that Armour Disaster Recovery was scheduled to present their case through lunch. But that had been before Ramon's outburst. The Chair did not like emotion. Jack sympathised—and knew when to cut his losses.

He rose to his feet. 'Thank you, Madam Chair.'

Ramon Lopez stared up at him in disbelief. 'We can't just *leave*. The committee—'

'Has our paper,' Jack supplied smoothly. He took hold of Ramon's chair behind his back and gave it a sharp tug. 'And of course we will be available to answer any questions that they have. You have my number?'

The Chair consulted the business cards she had set out in front of her place at the conference table. She was very professional.

'Yes, thank you, Dr Armour. I am sure we will have plenty of questions. It will be very helpful if you can keep yourself available.'

'You've got it,' said Jack. His charm was easy and quite false, though hopefully only Ramon detected it. He patted his pocket and looked round with a friendly smile. 'Thank God for mobile phones.'

The committee laughed uneasily, one eye on Ramon. It looked as if the passionate Spaniard was not going to move. They braced themselves for a nasty scene.

But Jack was not a personality it was easy to withstand and he was the boss. In the end, Ramon went. Muttering under his breath, but he went. He took the briefcase Jack thrust at him and followed him out of the room.

Once outside in the corridor, he let out an explosive breath.

'*Hell!* Why didn't I keep my mouth shut?'

Jack was checking that his mobile phone was switched on. He did not look up.

'You'll know better next time.'

'It's all my fault. I shouldn't have lost my temper. I should have used sweet reason, like you.'

Jack did look up then. His eyes gleamed with humour. 'Oh, I don't know. You sure impressed them when you thumped the table.'

Ramon was on the point of collapse. 'I have cost us everything. Everything.'

'Forget it,' said Jack at last, exasperated. 'We'll just have to manage the negotiations differently, that's all.'

Ramon shook his head wonderingly. 'Does anything ever faze you?'

Jack laughed. 'Every setback is an opportunity if you look at it the right way,' he said, maliciously quoting Ramon's favourite management guru.

Reluctantly Ramon smiled. 'Like the New York photographer who wants to take your portrait?' he retorted, malicious in his turn.

The Armour Recovery e-mail system had been buzzing with the tales of columnist Rita Caruso as the boss's latest conquest.

'Oh, you've got onto that one, have you?' said Jack, resigned.

Ramon's sense of humour was in recovery. 'Can't wait to see it.'

Jack snorted and put his telephone back in his pocket. 'You'll wait a long time.'

Ramon was all innocence. 'But you were the one who said we needed publicity.'

'Not that sort.'

'"Public awareness of the long-term effects of natural disasters is zero",' Ramon chanted.

It was the paragraph on donor fatigue from the report they had left with the committee. He had redrafted the paragraph a zillion times until Jack was satisfied with it. So he knew it by heart, as he now demonstrated.

'"After the immediate emergency, journalists move on. But more people die in the aftermath of most disasters than in the period of first impact. We must do everything we can to reverse this."' He smiled. 'Doesn't include some pretty pictures for a lady who fancies you?'

Jack cast his eyes to heaven. Or at least to the over-illuminated ceiling of the plushest corridor in Paris.

'Come on, man. I'll sell myself to a bunch of bureaucrats if that's what it takes to get the job

done. I draw the line at stud pics,' he said brutally.

Ramon was startled. '*Stud* pics?'

'Caruso's a photo-journalist with *Elegance*
magazine.'

'So?'

'They're only interested in fashion, sex and
gossip. Frankly, I was surprised they bothered to
send anyone along to Ignaz.'

Ramon stared. 'How do you know what
Elegance magazine is interested in? When did
you have time to read anything except work?'

Jack looked faintly uncomfortable. 'You only
have to look at the news-stands at airports.'

'Since when did you cruise the women's mag-
azines stands?' said Ramon in disbelief.

There was the tiniest pause. Then Jack said levelly, 'Susana liked it.'

For once Ramon had nothing to say.

To Holly, balancing her boxes like a circus pro,
the atmosphere between the two men blasted
down the corridor like a fireball. They were at the
far end, outside the board room. Two men in city
suits: one small and anxious, one tall and dark
and icily contained, as if holding his breath to
withstand a blow.

Holly was not quite sure how she knew he was bracing himself. His high-cheekboned face was impassive. But somehow she did. It was the way he stood. She had a vivid impression of a man using every ounce of strength to keep the lid on some inflammable substance and not being sure the lid would hold. It was alarming.

I'm glad it wasn't me who made him look like that, she thought, oddly shaken.

His companion said in English, 'I'm sorry, Jack. I didn't think. I'm an idiot.'

For a moment, the tall man did not answer. Then he said, 'Conference room fever.'

And she knew the moment of danger had passed.

His companion did not seem so sure. He looked up at the tall man doubtfully.

'In fact, look on the bright side. At least you've got us out of another forty-eight hours in there.'

Holly put one hand up to steady her precarious tower of boxes and marched towards them.

'Forty-eight hours?' The other man echoed, horrified. 'Oh, Jack, surely it won't take that long.'

Holly realised something else about the tall, intimidating stranger. He was gorgeous. Tough, yes; dangerously controlled, undoubtedly. But, beyond argument, gorgeous.

She frowned. Holly did not like gorgeous men. For very good reasons.

'I knew I'd made them mad. But forty-eight hours?'

Gorgeous Jack was cynical. 'Once you let bureaucrats start talking, it will last until they go home.'

The smaller man groaned. 'If only we didn't have to do this.'

Jack gave a sudden snort of laughter. 'What we need is a friendly millionaire who believes in forward planning. Failing that, the International Disaster Committee is the best we've got.'

Holly had reached them.

'Excuse me,' she said from behind her boxes.

She was standing at Jack's shoulder. The boxes tilted, catching against the canvas bag she wore looped across her body. She compensated, tilting in the other direction. Which might have made her voice muffled. Or maybe they were just too engrossed in their own affairs to notice.

Either way, they did not hear her.

'If only I hadn't put their backs up,' said the second man wretchedly.

'Not difficult with bureaucrats. They—'

'Excuse *me*.'

'—play status games all the—' Jack swung round impatiently. 'What is it?'

His eyes glittered like black diamonds. Holly was transfixed. Even with her boxes rocking off balance, she could not wrest her eyes away.

Gorgeous was not the word. And her instincts were sound: he looked hard, all right. The bone structure was that of a Greek god and, by the look of it, so was the temper. She could imagine people quailing under the intensity of that hooded gaze.

Well, she did not quail easily. She shifted her burden to one side and glared right back at him.

'May I get past?'

Fierce dark eyes swept over her like a forest fire.

Most people would have blenched. Holly congratulated herself on the difference between herself and most people. She also congratulated herself on not folding up against the wall of the corridor and trying to squeeze meekly past them.

She tapped her foot, to the imminent danger of her boxes.

'Now. Please.' It was still just polite. Technically, anyway.

For a moment, Gorgeous Jack surveyed Holly with unnerving concentration.

Holly had always been quick to flare up, even before she'd honed her defensive skills in the battlefield that was her father's house. Now her tem-

per went onto a slow burn. She stopped pretending to be polite.

'*Now!*'

To her fury, he was more alert than she was.
He was already moving when Holly felt the boxes
finally shift out of balance. Before they could top-
ple, he had swept round and lifted them out of
her arms.

He looked down at her, waiting.

'Thank you,' she said. She sounded as if she
were being strangled.

His mouth twitched. 'You're welcome.' But he
did not let the incident interrupt his real interest.
Over the top of the boxes, he said to his companion, 'Don't beat up on yourself, Ramon.'

Ramon hardly seemed to notice Holly. He was
frowning and clearly full of guilt.

'I should have let you handle it. I flew off the
handle.'

Jack shrugged elegantly suited shoulders. The
movement, Holly saw with fury, did not even stir
the pile of boxes he was holding.

'You lost focus. Can happen to anyone.' He
sent Holly a brief, indifferent glance. 'Where are
these supposed to go?'

Holly tried to feel grateful. It was not easy.

'The front desk said it was the office at the
end,' she muttered.

The tall man turned without a word.

'They're for some guy called Armour.' But she was talking to his back.

Great, she thought. *Stand back, you poor creature, and let a big strong man take control.* She had a long and justified prejudice against masterful men, too. She could have kicked him.

The man called Ramon pattered along beside him, taking two steps to every long stride.

'But surely they still can't keep us hanging about here for forty-eight hours?' He sounded as if he was about to burst into tears.

'They can try.'

Jack came to the impressive double doors at the end of the corridor and shouldered his way in without even a token knock. Nor, noted Holly, did he bother to acknowledge anyone in the secretariat that he had just invaded.

He dropped the boxes on the nearest desk and said generally, 'Is that where you want them?'

Holly was tempted, childishly, to say no it wasn't. Fortunately, the room's elegant chief occupant took charge before Holly could go to war.

She rose and rushed forward, flustered out of her professional calm.

'Oh, Mr Armour. I didn't realise... Yes, there would be fine.'

Holly realised she knew her. Señora Martinez had ordered in from Chez Pierre before. She was multilingual, super-efficient and famously unflappable.

She did not look unflappable now. One casual look from those fierce dark eyes and she was stammering like a schoolgirl.

'There are messages... The Director was asking... But I thought you'd still be with the committee...'

Holly watched in astonishment. Gorgeous Jack must be quite something, she thought. Señora Martinez was normally a Madonna of calm.

Now he said cheerfully, 'The committee threw us out, Elena.'

No sign now of that fury Holly had surprised in the corridor. In fact, he was smiling at Señora Martinez with such conscious charm it set Holly's teeth on edge.

It worked though. Señora Martinez laughed, blushed and shook her head at him.

'I'm sure they did no such thing, Mr Armour. I know they were all very impressed by your company's proposal.'

Holly did not like being ignored. The man had not spared her a glance since that flicker of amusement in the corridor. Now she seized upon the name.

'Armour, huh?' She placed herself in front of him and said loudly, 'Lunch for ten.'

He was blank. 'What?'

Silently she held the delivery docket out to him.

At least he looked at her then. He was impatient. He did not take the docket. But he looked.

'Yes?' If it was possible to sound more indifferent, Holly could not imagine it.

She could have danced with fury.

The trouble was, she knew what he was seeing and it was not impressive. The white buttoned chef's jacket was grubby after a morning's rapid deliveries through this busy part of Paris. And the baseball cap that covered her unruly golden-brown hair was frankly tatty.

She stuck her chin in the air and stood her ground. 'I want a signature for the delivery,' she said truculently, adding with a respect that was as unconvincing as it was belated, 'sir.'

The man's eyes narrowed, arrested. Señora Martinez looked shocked.

'My good child—' his voice was a drawling insult '—what in hell would I do with lunch for ten?'

Holly's temper went through the top of her head.

She said sweetly, 'I don't care if you take every single piece of quiche Lorraine and feed it to the pigeons. I want my signature.'

He had a long curly mouth. It made him look mocking without even trying.

'On the contrary. You want *my* signature. And believe me, no one gets that without working for it.'

Holly ground her teeth.

Señora Martinez intervened fast. 'Here is a misunderstanding.' Her perfect English was slipping under stress. 'The food is for the Committee's meeting with Mr Armour. It is I who ordered it.' She grabbed the docket and leaned it against her knee to scribble a signature.

Holly hardly looked at her.

'Mr Armour's meeting?' she said, letting her eyes drift up and down his tall figure with barely disguised scorn. 'Well, God bless America.'

Señora Martinez and Ramon exchanged alarmed glances. Gorgeous Jack, by contrast, began to look as if he was enjoying himself.

'Oh? Why?'

'The only nation in the world,' said Holly quoting her employer, gourmet chef Pierre, 'to make eating at the conference table a moral imperative.'

There was a startled silence. Holly pulled the peak of her baseball cap down defiantly.

The Greek god certainly looked like the sort of man who would refuse to permit lunch-breaks until the world fell into line. Yet somehow, with those unreadable eyes fixed on her, Holly felt as if she had made a very big mistake. And a complete fool of herself into the bargain.

Then he shrugged, confirming all Holly's prejudices about his nationality and his indifference to food.

'So I'm the king of the carry-out. What does that make you?'

Holly stared, taken aback.

'I guess you don't like the stuff,' he suggested. 'You just sell it.'

Oh, he was so confident, so pleased with himself, all high slanting cheekbones and black laughter. She had seen arrogance like that before.

Her brother-in-law and his best crony, the guy who ran her father's company, had both been like that. So certain that they were right; so certain that the awkward, illegitimate newcomer would realise it in the end and fall into line. Suddenly Holly wanted to scream at all of them. She wanted to so much she choked on it.

He smiled. 'Game, set and match to the slob who gets the pizza, huh?' And turned away.

Behind her Ramon laughed. 'Ouch.'

Holly flushed furiously. She could feel her ears tingle with it. There was a microsecond when she wanted to throw things, make him eat his words, make him *look* at her. Look and see more than a delivery robot.

Then the practical Holly reasserted herself. Reluctantly she curbed her temper. Pierre would never forgive her if she kicked a client. He might even sack her and she needed the job. She would have to get out of there before the temptation to hit him became overwhelming.

She almost snatched the docket from Señora Martinez and stuffed it into the canvas bag. It was full of flyers for the club where she worked in the evening. She was supposed to be circulating them. She had almost forgotten until now. With a gasp of guilt, she looked at her watch, clutched the bag to her and fled.

Another black mark in a bad, bad day.

First, a late night playing the flute at Le Club Thaïs had made her oversleep. Then there had been a delay on the Metro. By the time she'd got to work Chef Pierre had been growling with fury over intruders who interrupted his baking, the phone had been ringing off the wall and no one had even started to make up the day's orders.

And then, to cap it all, a tall dark stranger who looked as if he'd just stepped out of a dream, had scored an easy point off her because she'd let her temper out of its cage.

No more temper, Holly vowed, punching the elevator button as if it were a personal enemy. 'No more smart remarks.'

'A message from the Chair, Mr Armour.'

Señora Martinez was wary as she handed over a sheet of paper. The Chair always said Jack Armour was a tough negotiator but Elena Martinez had never seen him anything other than charming before. She did not know why he had challenged the young delivery girl like that. She felt sorry for her.

Jack opened the paper and scanned it rapidly.

'You and I,' he told Ramon in a dry voice, 'have got the afternoon off. The committee does not want us back.'

Ramon looked as if he might cry.

Elena Martinez said helplessly, 'But of course you are welcome to…' She gestured at the boxes Holly had brought.

Jack grinned suddenly. 'No, thanks. We'll pass on the picnic. The committee can have our share.' He buffeted Ramon lightly between the shoulder blades. 'No need to look like that. We can go play, now.'

Roman protested. 'But the committee, the contract…'

Jack laughed aloud. 'The committee has my mobile number and the contract is on the table. They can call when they're willing to sign.'

On which magnificent announcement, he swept Ramon out of the office and into the elevator.

'We should have stuck around,' objected Ramon as they descended to the ground floor. 'We should have gatecrashed that bloody committee again. We should—'

'Cool it, Ramon.'

'But—'

'Wait until we get out of the building.'

'What?'

Jack cast a meaning look at the closed-circuit camera above their head. Ramon subsided.

Jack tapped his fingers on the wood panelling.

'I've had three months up to my neck in mud and bureaucracy. I can use some major frivolity. Paris is good for that.'

Ramon hunched his shoulders. 'What sort of frivolity?'

'Good food, great wine, music.'

'That means you're going to cut the Combined Agencies' dinner,' Ramon diagnosed gloomily. 'I'll have to do it on my own again. You know I hate these things.'

Jack was unimpressed. 'Take a date.'

'Who do we know in Paris?'

Jack chuckled. 'You could always ask the chairperson. She was impressed by your Latin charm.'

'I couldn't—' Ramon began in lively alarm. Then he saw Jack's expression and relaxed. 'Take a date yourself. Then I can have the night off for once.'

Jack did not stop smiling. But suddenly it did not reach his eyes any more.

Hell, thought Ramon. Good score, Ramon. Second time in half an hour.

To cover his discomfort, he said roughly, 'That kid who brought the food—you should have got her number instead of beating up on her. Then you'd have a date yourself.'

Jack shook his head. 'Too much of a fighter.' But at least he was smiling again as if he meant it. 'I wonder who she really was?'

'What?'

They were getting out of the elevator. Ramon looked back at the camera, suddenly worried. 'Do you think she was some sort of spy? Political? Industrial? What?'

Jack laughed. 'Hey. Calm down. No one spies on the guys who put up tents at disaster sites.'

'But back in the elevator you said—'

'Back there I didn't want you bad-mouthing the committee. It would undoubtedly get back.'

'What do you mean?'

'Security guards rent out embarrassing bits of the surveillance tapes.'

Ramon stared, torn between affront and suspicion. 'I don't believe it.'

Jack shrugged.

'How do you know?' said Ramon, half convinced in spite of himself.

'I've done my time as a security guard.'

And that Ramon did believe. He knew that Jack had done every non-career job going while he was trying to get Armour Disaster Recovery off the ground.

'Though never in a state-of-the-art building like this.'

Jack looked round the entrance hall with a wry smile. Trees wafted in the air conditioning. There was a faint tinkle from a baroque fountain. The marble walls gleamed. Palms were everywhere. Among them, almost unnoticed, a steady stream of people arrived, departed, delivered, left messages. Their heels clipped on the floor. Their voices were lost in the cathedral-high atrium. And not one of them took any notice of anybody else in the flow.

Ramon shuddered. 'Give me mud every time.'

Jack nodded. 'Not exactly human size, is it?'

'Big enough to get lost in—'

But Ramon was talking to himself. As he stared, open-mouthed, Jack suddenly wasn't there any more. He had cast away his briefcase and was sprinting across the mirror-tiled floor.

Bewildered, Ramon fielded the briefcase and tried to see what had grabbed Jack's attention. The crowd streamed around him, oblivious.

And then Ramon saw.

It was the fiery delivery girl. She had lost her baseball cap and was backed up against a marble wall. A tall man was towering over her. He seemed to be shouting but his voice was lost in the echoing hall.

The girl did not seem to be following him anyway. Her eyes were quite blank. Terror, thought Ramon.

He had seen enough terror to recognise it easily, even across a crowded cathedral-sized entrance hall. So had Jack. Ramon knew exactly how Jack would react to the frozen panic on the girl's face.

'Oh, Lord,' said Ramon. He stuffed Jack's briefcase under his arm and pelted after him.

Jack was tall and fit as an athlete after the last three months' physical demands. But the girl's opponent was built like a prize fighter with huge shoulders and a neck like a bull's. Jack should not have been any match for him. But Jack had him in an arm lock in three short, vicious movements.

Ouch, thought Ramon who knew what Jack was capable of in one of his rare fits of fury. He speeded up.

'That's enough.' Ramon grabbed Jack's arm and hung onto it. He meant to sound authoritative but it came out like a plea.

Jack looked down at him as if he had forgotten where he was. He shook his head a little, as if to clear it. Then looked at the man in his grip.

'Who are you?'

The man choked out something indecipherable. He put up his hands to ease the pressure on his throat. Jack relaxed his grip a little.

'What makes you can think you can push women around?' Jack rapped out.

The man's chest heaved. He looked furious—and bewildered.

Beyond them, the girl straightened slowly. The black panic left her face but she still looked frighteningly young and vulnerable. A loose golden-brown plait fell forward over her shoulder.

She was panting. 'He has no right. He's nothing to do with me.' Her voice was suddenly very young, too.

The man was conventionally handsome, with chiselled features and expensively styled hair. But when he turned his head to look at her, his expression was as ugly as a street-corner punk's.

'Oh, no? I've got a piece of paper that says I'm your guardian.'

She flinched. But she did not deny it.

'Great,' muttered Ramon. Aloud, he said soothingly, 'Jack, these people don't want us interfering in their private affairs...'

Jack ignored him. He looked at the girl. 'Well?'

'He's married to—a relation of mine,' she said in a hurried, uneven voice. 'I don't ask them for anything. I don't want to have anything to do with them.' Her voice rose. It was quiet enough but it had the intensity of a scream.

Ramon winced. He was not surprised that Jack did not let the man go.

The man let out a roar of frustration that at last attracted the attention of one of the security guards. He ignored Jack and Ramon. 'You owe Donna,' he said. 'You know it. I know it.'

It sounded menacing, even to a stranger. The girl whitened. Her sudden pallor revealed a dusting of golden freckles across her nose.

The security guard began to stroll over. Jack was still holding the attacker in an arm lock. The girl looked past the man, straight at Jack, her hands twisting.

'I don't. I don't owe anyone. I never asked... Please...' Her voice was all over the place.

Jack said, 'Your guardian?'

She looked at the man, though it was easy to see that she did not want to meet his eyes. 'Brendan, please don't do this.' It was obviously a huge effort to speak with even an attempt at calm. 'I don't want anything from you. I never have. I just want to be *free*.'

Jack's face was a mask.

Oh, Lord, that's torn it, thought Ramon.

Jack said slowly, 'How old are you?'

'T-twenty-two.'

He looked at the big man in his grip. 'No one has a guardian at twenty-two.'

'You do if—'

But the girl was not waiting any longer. The security guard reached them. They all turned to him instinctively, the tight little circle round the girl widening for a moment. She saw her chance and took it. She dived between Ramon and Jack so fast that she knocked Ramon flying. In seconds, she was out through the revolving doors.

Jack's captive swore. He would have taken off after her if Jack had not wrestled him up against the wall and held him there.

'I think not,' Jack said very softly.

'But that girl is my ward.'

'She doesn't seem to think so.'

'I tell you—'

'And I tell you, ward or no ward, you will not manhandle her while I'm here to stop you.'

There was a steely note to Jack's voice which brought the hairs up on the back of Ramon's neck. Even the stranger seemed to recognise that this was not a man he could bully. Some of the bluster left him.

He took refuge in sarcasm. 'Sweet little Holly done a number on you too, has she?'

Jack did not answer.

The man tried to push his restraining hand away and failed.

'That's a real good act she's got,' he sneered. 'Can't tell you the number of guys she took in back home in Lansing Mills. That was why she ran out—'

Jack stopped him with a gesture of disgust. 'Enough, already.'

The security guard decided to intervene at last. He had checked Jack Armour into the committee many times and trusted him. The other man, however, was new to him. Mindful of the fat folder of guidelines under the reception desk, he asked some slow and careful questions. By the time

Ramon had appointed himself interpreter and translated them from French, the girl was long gone.

Jack let go of his captive. After a brief struggle with frustration, the man came up with his answers readily enough.

'My name is Brendan Sugrue.' He produced a passport from his back pocket. 'That girl is my sister-in-law. By adoption. My wife and I are her legal guardians. We are from Lansing Mills, Oklahoma. She ran away. I have been on her trail ever since.'

'Why?' said Jack. It was quiet enough but it had the force of a bullet.

The security guard looked up curiously from his perusal of the passport.

Brendan Sugrue blinked. 'She's young…'

'Twenty-two-year-olds can take care of themselves.

'Unstable…'

Jack's eyes narrowed almost to slits. 'In what way?'

'Irresponsible. Wild. She doesn't listen to advice…'

He saw Jack's expression. His words dwindled into silence.

'Doesn't listen to advice, huh? Sounds like she doesn't do what you want,' said Jack softly.

'Monsieur Armour,' began the security guard, friendly but minatory.

Jack ignored him.

'Isn't that the truth of it?'

'Monsieur Armour, this is clearly a personal matter.' The guard returned the passport. 'As the young lady has gone and no damage has been done, there is no more to be said. Goodbye, gentlemen.'

Brendan Sugrue shook himself. Then he straightened his tie and brushed out the creases in his elegant jacket.

'Thank you,' he said to the security guard. The look he sent Jack was less friendly. 'I'd hoped to clear this up informally. Thanks to your meddling, I'll probably have to go to the police now. Don't get in my way again.'

He shouldered his way past Jack and Ramon. The force with which he slammed out of the building sent the revolving doors spinning.

The guard pulled a face. 'Hope the young lady is a long way away by now,' he said, all his French chivalry aroused.

'Hope we don't get involved,' muttered Ramon, less chivalrous but infinitely more practical.

The pristine floor was scattered with litter. Jack scuffed some with his shoe and then looked down, arrested. To Ramon's astonishment he fell to his knees and began picking up several dozen bright yellow sheets of coarse paper.

'Now what?'

Jack held a sheet up to him.

'"Club Thaïs",' read Ramon. '"Cool jazz, hot beat".' He turned it over. On the back there was a menu. He cast a knowledgeable eye over the prices. 'Just some cheap brasserie. What about it?'

Jack picked up the rest of the flyers. 'She dropped them.'

Ramon's heart sank. 'So?'

'So maybe she goes there. Works there, even.'

'Or maybe she works for an agency which delivers flyers and she's never been over the threshold,' said Ramon discouragingly.

Jack stood up and retrieved his briefcase.

'Nowhere this cheap employs agencies for anything,' he said, stuffing the retrieved papers into his case.

'OK. Maybe her boyfriend is a waiter there.'

Jack stopped.

'Most twenty-two-year-old girls,' pointed out Ramon, sensing an advantage, 'have boyfriends.' As Jack still said nothing he ploughed on. 'Look, who knows the rights and wrongs of this? Maybe

Sugrue is right and the girl is nuts. We really don't need you playing St George again.'

Their eyes met for a long, comprehending moment. Ramon's were the first to fall. Third time today, he thought. Well done, Ramon.

'I'm sorry,' he said. 'Jack, I'm real sorry.'

'Yes,' said Jack, expressionless.

'But she can look after herself. You saw that. First chance she had, she took off. And that guy won't catch her off guard again. She'll be keeping an eye out for him.'

'Not much doubt of that.' Jack's tone was light but there was a small muscle working in his cheek. 'She looked like she wasn't going to stop running for a week.'

Ramon knew that tell-tale muscle all too well. He said desperately, 'Nothing to do with us.'

Jack just looked at him.

'We're only here for another two days.' Ramon's voice rose. 'What could you do in two days? You don't even know her *name*.'

Jack stirred the remaining yellow litter with his foot. 'But I've got a clue. And a good deductive brain. And time on my hands until the committee makes its call.'

'You're going to go looking for her?'

Jack's mouth twisted in self-mockery. 'I'm going to follow my instincts.'

Ramon flung up his hands. 'You're crazy.'

'Maybe.'

The mockery died, leaving only determination. Ramon had seen Jack look like that before. He gave up.

CHAPTER TWO

HOLLY raced out of the building and pelted blindly for the Métro. She could lose herself in the crowd that always filled the busy station.

It was only when she was halfway down the steps that she remembered she was supposed to be in charge of Chef Pierre's little van. Before taking the boxes up to the committee floor, she had parked illegally in the forecourt of the building. She knew that the attendant turned a blind eye to short-stay catering vans at lunchtime. But if she left it there for much longer he would have it towed away.

She stopped. The man behind bumped into her hard. Holly's heart lurched and she gave a small scream. But then she turned and saw that he was a complete stranger. Muttering something uncomplimentary, he pushed past her and ran down into the darkness of the Métro.

Holly put a hand to her heart. It still thudded like a power drill. But at least she had her head back together.

She toiled back up the steps into the spring sunshine. Calm down, she told herself. This is

Paris, not Lansing Mills. Brendan won't have the police dancing to his tune here. And even Brendan won't kidnap me in the public street.

But she still looked round warily when she went back to collect the van. To her huge relief, there was no sign of Brendan Sugrue. Or of her rescuer. That, she was affronted to discover, was no relief at all. In fact, she was definitely disappointed.

'But it's just as well,' said Holly aloud. 'I don't need Gorgeous Jack to look after me.'

She got into the ancient van and fumbled the ignition comprehensively. The engine flooded. Holly pounded her fists on the wheel.

'I don't need anyone to look after me,' she raged.

She turned the key again. The engine gave a tubercular cough and died. There was nothing to do but wait.

And think. And remember.

Oddly, it was not Brendan she remembered; not his schemes and manipulation and, when that failed, his bullying. Nor the claustrophobic world of Lansing Mills. Not even her father's successor with his manicured hands and dead eyes—the eyes that had ultimately stampeded her into bolting for freedom. What she remembered, what she could not get out of her head, was an impatient man with a long sexy mouth and an air of ineffable superiority.

Gorgeous Jack would not have flooded the engine of the temperamental little van, thought Holly, seething. He would have lit the spark at his first attempt. Then he would have driven off with any woman he rescued safe beside him...

'*Stop right there.* I don't need to be rescued,' Holly told the dashboard, glaring. 'I haven't needed anyone to rescue me for the last five years. I don't need anyone now. Particularly not a superior clown in an Armani suit. I *don't.*'

But as she finally switched on the engine and drove out into the boulevard, she could not quite banish Jack Armour's dark, dark eyes. Or the thought that it would be heaven to have a man like that take over the fight against Brendan.

Now that, thought Holly fervently, I *really* can't afford. Put it out of your mind, girl.

She tried. She really tried.

By the time she got to work that evening she had almost succeeded. She slipped into Club Thaïs half an hour after it opened. She came via the fire escape, not for the first time.

'You're late,' said Gilbert, the owner. He followed her into the tiny cupboard under the stairs where the staff left their belongings. 'The husband catching up?'

He would have been cautious about tangling with an uncertain law. But, as Holly had soon worked out, he was a hundred per cent in favour of running away from a bad marriage. So she had told him what he wanted to hear, that any man who turned up looking for her would be her jealous ex-husband. So Gilbert, a frustrated romantic, was happy to help cover her tracks.

Holly half closed the cupboard door against him. In cramped modesty, she shrugged out of her denim jacket and T-shirt and pulled a black cropped top over her head. 'Uh-huh.'

Gilbert was not very interested in her personal life. 'How many flyers did you deliver?' he said from his stance in the hallway.

'Got rid of the lot,' said Holly, conveniently forgetting that half her load had scattered themselves over the floor.

She slithered into the black jeans that all Gilbert's staff wore, even if, like Holly, they jammed in with the musicians from time to time.

She pushed the cupboard door open and emerged to find Gilbert vainly polishing steam off the wall mirror. He turned, smiling.

'Good. We need some new punters. It's slow tonight.'

Not bothering to look in the mirror, she flattened the wisps of hair which escaped from her plait with quick, expert fingers.

'It may hot up when Tobacco start their set,' she said comfortingly.

Tobacco—'this band can seriously damage your health'—were new and cool and the club's patrons loved them. Not much chance of jamming in tonight, thought Holly, storing her flute carefully behind the discarded clothes.

'If that happens, I'll need you to stay late again. OK?'

Holly nodded. That meant good tips and, if Gilbert was feeling generous, a bonus in her take-home cash. If she was going on the run again she would need it. Brendan did not look as if he was open to negotiation—or about to give up.

She looked quickly at the blackboard behind the chef's head and memorised the menu with the speed of long practice. There were not that many changes to the food at the Club Thaïs. People came to talk, to dance, to drink and, sometimes, to listen to the jazz. The meal was strictly incidental.

For a moment, Holly was sad. The Club Thaïs had been a home from home for her for ten months now. She would miss it.

But there was no point in wasting time on regrets—not about going on the run again; not about having seen the last of Gorgeous Jack. Every moment was for living, her mother had said. In the last five years Holly had come to believe it.

She grabbed her order pad and squared her shoulders against the world.

'OK, Gilbert, here we go,' she said gaily. She flung back the swing doors into the restaurant. 'Let the good times roll.'

'Why here? Oh God, you're following that girl, aren't you?'

Ramon stood at the top of the cellar steps and looked at the half-full cellar with distaste.

Jack's smile was bland.

'You said you wanted to see the real Paris.'

'Not this real.'

'Come on, Ramon. It's not like you to pass up a chance to let your hair down.'

'After we've clinched the deal. Not before. I don't want to go into an eight o'clock meeting with a hangover from bad wine and worse jazz.'

But Jack was unrelenting. 'Local colour,' he said hardily. 'Savour the experience.'

Grumbling, Ramon followed him down into the dark of the club. The floor was made up of uneven stone flags and the walls, as far as the low lighting allowed them to be seen, were covered in posters for poetry readings and obscure bands.

They sat at a rickety corner table. It was covered with a square of rigid paper and bore half a candle in a chipped saucer.

'Very ethnic,' said Ramon sourly.

About half the tables were full. A thin man was making concentrated music with the tabla and there was a desultory hum of conversation. Jack ordered a bottle of red wine and then sat back and surveyed the crowd alertly.

'You look like you're waiting for something.'

'Maybe we're about to hear the new Duke Ellington,' said Jack. His voice was lazy, but his eyes were not.

Ramon was dubious. 'Maybe...' And then he sat bolt upright. 'Oh, no.'

'What?'

'*Damn.*'

'Where is she? said Jack, lazy no longer. His eyes were searching the cellar, hard and intent.

'Jack, *think—*'

Jack ignored him. He raised a hand to the waiter and when the man came over said, 'The young waitress. The one with the long plait. What's her name?'

The waiter looked at him suspiciously. 'Holly,' he said.

'Holly what?'

The waiter shrugged.

'Does she work here regularly?'

'Why don't you ask her? Hey, Hol. Over here.'

She wove her way between the tables. 'Yes? Can I—?' She broke off.

It was him. *Him.* Her heart went into a nose-dive.

Jack stood up.

Her heart levelled out and started to tap-dance.

'It's you,' said Holly not much above a whisper.

It was unbelievable. As if by thinking about him, she had conjured him up like a genie. Perhaps he wasn't really there, except in her imagination? She shook her head trying to clear it. But even after that he was still there.

Oh, yes, there all right. Tall and dark and just as gorgeous as she remembered.

The waiter knew the story she had told Gilbert. He tensed, suspicious. Holly knew, even though she did not take her eyes off Jack.

'It's all right, Marc,' she said hurriedly. 'Mr Armour and I met earlier today.'

Marc shrugged and went.

Holly did not move. She felt turned to stone and tongue-tied into the bargain. She looked down at her order pad as if she did not know what it was for.

Jack said, 'Won't you join us?'

She swallowed. 'I can't. I'm working.'

But she did not go.

'Holly,' Jack said. It sounded as if he was tasting it.

Holly felt a convulsive shiver run through her—deep and dark and utterly unfamiliar. It bewildered her. She raised her eyes to his face. With a little shock she realised that he recognised what she was feeling.

She blinked, struck to silence. No one had ever looked at her like that before—as if he knew her every last secret sensation.

He said her name again, so softly that only she could hear it.

'Holly who?'

His eyes bored into her. The noisy little club seemed to recede, leaving just the two of them alone. Holly opened her mouth but no sound came out of it.

'You know my name, after all,' he prompted.

His determination beat at her like a high wind. He did not smile. Holly had never felt such force of will.

Get a grip, she told herself feverishly. *Get a grip.*

She moistened her lips. 'I don't tell my name to strangers.'

He did smile then. It was the same smile as this afternoon—cool and superior, as if he was so certain he was right he did not have to bother to prove it. Quite suddenly Holly's sense of unreality evaporated like a burst bubble.

'Hardly a stranger. I took on a guy for you today and stopped him cold.'

'I didn't ask you to,' she flashed.

'Are you saying you wish I hadn't?'

She sidestepped that. 'I don't approve of violence.'

'And you wish I hadn't?' he persisted.

She tilted her chin. 'I run my own life, right? If you hadn't come along, I would have dealt with Brendan.'

'It looked like it,' he said drily.

'I've done it before.'

He looked sceptical. 'Successfully?'

Holly shifted. She was too innately honest to claim success in her dealings with Brendan Sugrue. She was all too aware that her strategy consisted mainly of running away whenever Brendan appeared over the horizon. But she was not willing to admit it to this masterful stranger.

Jack saw her hesitation and pressed home his advantage. 'So if he turns up here tonight, you don't need my help?'

'Tonight?'

In spite of her brave words, Holly flinched at the thought. She could not help it. She looked nervously at the staircase from the entrance.

'That was a nasty incident this afternoon,' Jack said more gently. 'Don't beat up on yourself. Most people can't handle physical threats.'

Holly gave him a long look. 'But you can?'

'I've had a lot of practice.'

'And that's supposed to reassure me?'

He was taken aback for a moment. She saw it in his eyes and felt a small glow of achievement.

Then he said, 'Are you telling me you don't need me on your side?'

All the lovely triumph drained away, exposing her weakness with horrible clarity. Remembering Brendan's ugly expression, Holly had a moment of pure fear.

At Jack's elbow, Ramon murmured a protest. Neither of them paid any attention to him.

Jack's face was hard. 'Tell me you don't need me and I'll go.'

There was a sudden, odd silence. Their eyes locked. Holly felt stunned but had no idea why.

She was as out of breath as if she had been running.

Jack's eyes flared, then narrowed to slits. She had the oddest feeling that he was even more startled than she was. Startled and not at all pleased.

She did not understand any of it. But she was certainly not going to say that she needed Gorgeous Jack Armour. Not for anything. Not ever.

Sidestepping the issue neatly, she said, 'You really think he'll come here tonight?'

Jack shrugged. 'If I found you, he can.'

She looked round the room. It was filling up but there was no one who looked like Brendan. Though she saw now that Gilbert was waving imperatively from the kitchen doorway.

'I've got to get on with my work,' said Holly, distracted.

'I don't hound women. Tell me to go and I will.'

Their eyes clashed. Locked.

Holly tore her gaze away and sought desperately for something to get her off the hook. She spied the bottle on their table.

'You don't have to go. You're a paying customer.' She began to back away. 'Finish your wine.'

'Oh, no,' said Jack. He had not moved a step but she felt as if he was pursuing her like her own personal Fate. 'I'm not here for the wine and you know it.'

Holly met his eyes straight on. 'So what are you here for?' She flung it at him like a challenge. 'Me?'

His eyes flickered.

'And you say you don't hound women?'

The sexy mouth thinned to a fierce line. He said harshly, 'I stopped a nasty piece of bullying this afternoon.'

'That doesn't give you any rights—'

'Maybe not. But it gives me some unfinished business.'

Holly was taken aback. She lost hold of her protective fury in sheer bewilderment. 'What are you talking about?'

'Mr Sugrue told me not to get in his way again,' Jack said thoughtfully.

For a moment Holly did not understand. Then, 'And that means you have to do whatever he told you not to? Was it some sort of challenge? You can't leave it alone?'

There was a tiny pause. 'Something like that.'

She shivered. 'I shall never understand men.'

He shrugged. 'Let's just say, I decided to stay on the case. But it's your case.' His eyes were intent. 'If you don't want me to, I'm gone.'

The silence demanded an answer.

Cornered, resentful, Holly was forced into honesty. 'No. Don't go.' It sounded as if it was dragged out of her.

'*Holly,*' bawled Gilbert.

'I've got to go...'

Jack said pleasantly, 'No problem,' and sat down quite as if she had begged him to stay and he had graciously acceded.

Holly could have screamed.

But Gilbert was becoming too urgent to ignore. With a last look of frustration at Jack, she threaded a quick path through the tables.

'Take your apron off,' said Gilbert, too preoccupied to be angry. 'Tobacco are going to be late and Jerry is finishing now. Get your flute.'

Left at the table, Ramon let out a long breath. 'Whew. For a moment, I thought she had you on the run there.'

Jack sat back with a faint smile. 'I knew she was a fighter,' he said. He sounded pleased about it.

'Well, you certainly got her mad.'

'Yes,' said Jack, his eyes glinting. 'I did, didn't I?'

Ramon gave up. 'Let's eat.'

They had finished their rough pâté and were waiting for a Moroccan stew when a new musician walked onto the small dais. She had a long golden-brown plait over one shoulder and a gleaming silver flute in her hands.

Ramon, who was drinking his wine, spluttered. Jack remained unmoved. Though when she put the instrument to her lips and went into a long bluesy riff that made the instrument sound like a saxophone, his eyes narrowed.

'What's she doing that for?' muttered Ramon when he got his breath back.

Jack did not answer him. 'Versatile,' he mused.

He did not say anything else, though he listened with attention. Holly finished her solo. A keyboard player joined her and they went off on a wild ride that had enough salsa rhythms to persuade some of the crowd to push back their chairs and dance.

'Very versatile,' Ramon said drily. 'Sounds like a girl who's been taking care of herself for years, doesn't she?'

Jack did not answer. His face was unreadable. He turned his chair slightly so that, without actually diverting his attention from the musicians, he could keep an eye on the door at the top of the stairs.

Ramon sighed.

The cellar filled up. The staff slid between tables and dancers, carrying impossible burdens of plates of food and bottles and thick short glasses for the wine. The whole place began to hum. The music got louder.

'This is good,' shouted Ramon, enthusiastically mopping up the last of his stew with a piece of crusty baguette.

And so it was. The party atmosphere seemed to infect everyone except Jack. Holly, half dancing in her concentration, was oblivious of everything but her music. So no one noticed when the thick-set man came in and stood on the stairs for a minute, scanning the heaving cellar.

No one but Jack, that was. He was out of his seat before Ramon knew what was happening.

'Get a cab,' Jack flung over his shoulder, as he made for the musicians. 'Meet us out the back. Quickly.'

There were times when you did not argue with Jack. Ramon knew this was one of them. He went.

Holly was hot and her hair had started to stick to her neck. When Harry gave her the high sign that he was going into a solo, she lowered the flute with a grin of relief. There was a surge of uninhibited applause. She bowed, laughing.

But then a powerful hand took hold of her.

'Time to go.'

Alarmed, she swung round. But it was not Brendan. It was Jack. And he was holding her as if he owned her.

'Excuse *me*,' said Holly, brave on salsa and success.

He was impervious.

'The brother-in-law from hell just walked in,' he told her with a bland smile. 'Do you want to stand and fight? Or run?'

Now that Harry was playing, she might just as well not have been there as far as the audience was concerned. No one questioned Jack's possessive grip on her arm, Holly saw. Just as no one would question Brendan if he chose to...

She stood very still, suddenly no longer hot. Deep inside, she began to shiver in the convulsive, mind-blinding way she thought she had forgotten. And now remembered all too well.

Trying to think, she pushed a hand through the loosening hair at her temple.

'I don't know.' She sounded stupefied.

Jack was brisk. 'Well, make your mind up fast. He looks as if he knows he's come to the right place.'

She stared across the cavernous room. Brendan was still scanning the waiters. He had not focused on the musicians yet. He had never taken her music seriously. None of them had. She winced, stabbed by another painful shaft of memory.

And at that moment Brendan caught sight of her. He ran down the stairs and began to push his way between the tables, brushing waiters out of the way. He never took his eyes off her.

Panic gripped Holly. She could not think straight. She could not *move*.

She heard Jack give an exasperated exclamation. He half-pulled, half-carried her off the dais and through the swing doors into the kitchen.

'It's all right, kid,' he said under his breath. 'Hang on to me. I'll get you out.'

Gilbert was at the kitchen hatch. He made to bar their way.

'You've got a difficult customer out there,' Jack told him briefly. 'Stall him.'

One concerned look at Holly's dazed expression, and Gilbert fell back, nodding. The doors banged behind him as he bustled into the club.

Jack took the flute out of Holly's limp grasp and swept her up the stairs and into the alley. It was full of empty boxes and vegetable matter. The smell shocked her out of her frozen daze.

'My bag…'

'Pick it up tomorrow.'

She thought: He sounds as if he has done this before.

It was a startling thought; alarming, in one way. But Holly was beyond alarm and, anyway, there was a steady, unshockable capability about Gorgeous Jack that made you rely on him. Normally it would have set her teeth on edge. Now she was just thankful. She leaned into him, trying to pull herself together.

There was a car at the end of the alley. Holly saw a light on its roof and stiffened.

'Police...' she said under her breath.

Jack looked down at her, his eyes suddenly sharp.

'Taxi cab. I told Ramon to get one.'

He took her hand and ran her to the waiting car.

The Armour Disaster Recovery delegation was staying at a small hotel, immensely comfortable and almost impossible to find. Jack took her there without even asking her. Without asking, either, he booked a room for her and then took her into the small bar.

Holly huddled by the spring fire, her hands tight round the small strong coffee which was all she could be pushed into accepting.

Jack said, 'For the last time—Holly who?'

She gave in. 'Dent. Holly Dent.'

He nodded. To her surprise, there was no sign of triumph there. 'I think you have to tell me about it.'

She swallowed. 'My bag—' she said again. She felt as if she had lost her identity along with her canvas shoulder bag and an old tee shirt.

Jack looked at Ramon. The Spaniard sighed.

'I'll go back to the club and get it. Anything else?'

'My flute.'

'I brought that with me. It's behind the bar,' said Jack.

'Oh?' She gave a wavering smile. 'That's a relief. I wouldn't want Brendan to get his hands on it. He can be stupid sometimes.' She rubbed her shoulder unconsciously, as if she felt the shadow grip of a heavy hand.

Jack and Ramon exchanged glances. A muscle worked in Jack's jaw.

But all he said was, 'OK. Your bag. That's it?'

Holly shook her head helplessly. 'The flute case. The clothes I wore to work. Um—I can't think. Gilbert will know.'

Ramon nodded to Jack and went. Holly hardly seemed to notice.

Jack sat back in the tapestry chair and watched her carefully.

'Why does this man frighten you so much?' he said at last.

Holly jumped and came out of her unhappy reverie. She did not look at him. 'It's a long story.'

She was rubbing her shoulder again as if it hurt her. Jack watched. He had seen an unconscious movement like that before. He suspected he knew what it meant. Out of sight, his hands clenched.

But his voice was neutral, utterly uninvolved. 'Has he some hold over you? Legally?'

What a minefield that question was, thought Holly wearily. She sipped her coffee and said at last, 'Maybe.'

Jack was silent for an unnerving minute.

She lifted her chin. 'What?'

'I don't think it is very clever of you to play games with me,' he said softly. 'I'm not likely to help you if you don't tell me the truth. And at the moment I'd say I'm your best bet.'

Probably my only bet, thought Holly. If Brendan could track her down to the Club Thaïs so quickly, he could probably track her down anywhere she went. He must be making Donna throw money into the search.

Poor Donna! Not knowing her own father, she had clung to her stepfather. And then to find that he'd left his company to the blood daughter he had only just discovered! Donna had felt rejected, but Brendan was, quite simply, furious. And Donna, hurt, loving and blind, did what Brendan told her.

Holly shivered. Oh, yes, so much better to pack your heart in ice. And not let any man take you over.

'So?' prompted Jack.

Holly brought herself back to the present with an effort.

She selected quickly from the miserable complications of her personal history.

'I don't know whether he has any legal claim to be my guardian and that's the honest truth.'

Jack preserved an unimpressed silence.

'Look,' she said, half-exasperated, half-desperate, 'he is married to my stepsister. My parents died within a couple of years of each other—' and what a continent of complications she skipped over there '—and I ended up living with them.'

It telescoped a bit but it was basically true.

'That doesn't explain why you're afraid of him.'

Holly flinched.

'Well?'

Her eyes fell. 'We—er—didn't agree on my future. So I left.'

'What did you disagree about?'

That was the crux. Holly resolutely refused to admit the image of her father. She had an odd feeling that if she thought about him, Jack would know it. It was as if Jack were a mind-reader. Or could read *her* mind, at least.

She said woodenly, 'I wanted to continue my education.'

Jack's deep-set dark eyes bored into hers as if he were the judge and she were a criminal. Holly narrowed her own eyes and stared straight back at him defiantly.

'All right,' he said at last. He didn't sound as if he believed her; just as if he was letting it go for the moment. 'So how can he stop you? Money?'

She shook her head violently. 'No. I've never taken any money from them. I don't want any.'

She sounded as if the very idea filled her with horror, thought Jack. He stored the information away for future consideration.

'So—how can he have any hold over you? If you really are twenty-two.'

Quite suddenly, Holly laughed. Sweet and true and startlingly youthful, her laugh rang round the little bar, waking up the drowsy barman with its genuine amusement. Jack was surprised and, for once, it showed.

'You're probably right,' she said ruefully. 'Only they live in Smallville, USA, and my father left a crazy will. I know I ought to have challenged it. But, frankly, I wasn't ever going to convince a local court to see it my way.'

Jack raised his eyebrows. 'Why not? I should point out that I'm from Smallville, USA myself,' he said drily.

'Then I shouldn't need to explain,' retorted Holly. 'There isn't a lawyer in the county who would take me as a client in a case against the family. They're respected citizens.' Full of irony, her eyes met his. 'Which means big local employers. Pretty well the only employers.'

'Ah,' said Jack in immediate comprehension.

She sighed. 'It's understandable, I suppose. I was only seventeen and I'd lived in Lansing Mills for less than two years. Everyone had known Donna since before she was born. And Brendan since he married her. I suppose people thought they were just trying to take care of me. Stopping me doing silly things. All for my own good.' For a moment she looked unbearably sad.

Jack knew that look. He had seen it too many times. It was the look of a prisoner resigned to the trap she was in. It always turned something over in his stomach, making him rage, making him want to make the prisoner rage.

Instead he said woodenly, 'So you took the law into your own hands. You ran.'

The sad look dispelled. For a moment she looked naughty—and very young.

'Yup.'

'Why, exactly? Why then?'

She evaded that. 'My daddy left a will saying that Donna was to look after me until I'm twenty-five unless I get married.'

All the bright naughtiness vanished. She looked as if she were tasting poison.

Jack said slowly, 'And no one gets married at seventeen, right?'

She evaded that too. 'They thought that meant I should stay at home, not go to college or travel or anything. Donna,' she added, 'never travelled.'

'They were unkind to you?'

Holly stared into the fire.

'They wouldn't have thought so,' she said at last, carcfully.

Jack pondered in silence. 'You were afraid of that man this afternoon,' he said at last. 'I saw it.'

Holly's head reared up. Startled hazel eyes met his. They were unguarded for a moment and very, very wary.

And blazing.

'You don't trust me an inch,' Jack said on a note of discovery. 'Do you?'

Her lids fell, veiling the betraying expression. She gave a shrug.

'Why should I?'

He made an exasperated noise. 'I got you away from Brendan Sugrue. Twice.'

'Yes, you did,' she said coolly. 'I ask myself why.'

There was a blank silence. 'Not an inch,' Jack repeated.

She shrugged again. 'Why should I trust you?'

'Because you don't have many choices. And you need help.'

Her spine snapped vertical. 'No, I don't.'

He ignored that. 'What made you run away from home?'

Their eyes met: hers alarmed, furious; his impassive. Hers were the first to fall.

She said flippantly, 'I didn't like having to be in by ten.'

A longer silence this time. She turned her head away but his eyes never left her profile.

Then Jack said very softly, 'Why don't I believe you?'

The barman interrupted. 'Mr Armour. There is a phone call for you.'

Jack hesitated, not taking his eyes off her. Holly sat still under the raking inspection. But when he shrugged and went to the bar she sagged in the chair as if an interrogation light had been turned off.

Oh, boy, had she misjudged Jack Armour, she thought. Her mouth twisted in a wry smile. She did not often do that. She had learned to sum people up quickly. On the road, these last five years, her survival had depended on her getting it right.

Yet she had looked at Jack Armour and got him one hundred and eighty degrees wrong. She had seen all that overwhelming male confidence and dubbed him Gorgeous Jack. Oh, she was right about the confidence—those slanted, unreadable eyes; the arrogant handsome features; the air of contained *power*...

Sexy as hell, thought Holly dispassionately. She could manage dispassion now that he was at the bar with his back to her, talking hard into a telephone. Sexy as hell, but much, much more than that. He had known she was not telling him the whole truth. Most people did not. And no one, in her experience, had tried to make her spread out her secrets on a platter for inspection.

She had only just held out, too. In his own way Jack Armour was as determined as Brendan. In fact, he was almost as bad as Homer.

Holly caught herself. She gave a little superstitious shiver. No one was as bad as Homer, she reminded herself soberly. No one. That was why she had run in the first place. And why she was going to keep on running until she was twenty-five and none of Brendan's clever lawyers could find a way to pull her back.

Hang on to that, she told herself. *Two and a half more years to freedom. You've come this far. You can do the rest.*

CHAPTER THREE

JACK finished his phone call and came back to her.

'I've got to work,' he told her briefly.

Holly thought, *Work! That's all he's interested in. I'm getting in the way of it.*

She nodded, not looking at him. 'I'll wait for your friend to bring my things and then I'll go.'

Inexplicably, that did not please Jack. 'It will be late. And what if that guy has found out where you live?'

Holly could not help herself. She shuddered at the thought. But giving way to panic was no solution. She had learned that well over the last five years.

So she tilted her chin and said flippantly, 'I won't open the door.'

In spite of the fact that he should be working, Jack did not go. He tapped his foot impatiently. But he did not move from the spot.

'You could stay here.'

'No, I couldn't.'

'Why not? I've reserved a room for you.'

'Because I can't afford it,' Holly said patiently.

67

That tapping foot was mesmerising. He seemed full of pent-up energy. What would it be like if he caught her up in it? What would it be like if he was not involved with work and on the point of leaving? What if he touched—?

Holly caught her thoughts just as they were about to run away with her.

'I can't afford it,' she said again, not entirely referring to the room rate.

'I can.'

Holly stiffened. Her years on the road had taught her that offers of free bed and board seldom came without strings.

Jack read her mind, it seemed. His eyes darkened until they looked almost black.

'No need to look like that. I told you, I've got to *work* tonight.'

Holly felt a fool. She took refuge in indignation.

'Well, what was I supposed to think? Most guys want something in return.'

Their eyes locked. Holly could almost hear the clash of swords.

And more than that. For a moment, turbulent impatience came off him in waves. As if he could not wait to be off and was furious with himself for staying. As if he could not help himself.

She blinked, utterly disconcerted.

Jack's mouth thinned. 'You've been playing with the wrong guys,' he said curtly.

'I—'

He took no notice. 'Still, it's up to you. The room is there if you want it.'

'But—'

'No bill.' He was nearly spitting the words out. 'No payment in kind. Goodnight.'

And he was gone before she could think of one word to stop him.

'*Damn,*' said Holly with real feeling.

She had simmered down by the time Ramon got back with her things. He came into the bar bearing her flute case and an incongruous plastic bag with a dusty pair of jeans and her canvas satchel spilling out of it. Holly seized the bag and began to rummage.

Ramon felt in his jacket pocket. 'If you're looking for your passport, I've got it here.'

He gave her an odd look. Holly did not notice. She just grabbed the little booklet with relief.

'There was no money,' said Ramon conscientiously. 'Or keys.'

Holly grinned and pulled a slim fold of notes out of her back pocket. 'I never take more than running-away money to the club. As for my key—' She shook her wrist and Ramon saw that she wore a charm bracelet. A serviceable key was attached to it.

'Clever.' He did not sound very comfortable about it. He looked round. 'Where's Jack?'

Holly's cheerfulness faded. 'There was a phone call. He said he had to work.'

Ramon groaned. 'There goes another night's sleep. I'd better go and see what he wants me to do.' He hesitated, already halfway into the task. 'You OK?'

'I'm fine,' she said, as she had said to Jack. She had to be fine, she told herself. 'Er—I suppose Brendan had gone by the time you got there?'

'Oh. Yes. I don't think you need to worry. The people at the club all seem to be on your side.'

Ramon shifted uncomfortably. He had had a surprising conversation with Gilbert. He still did not know what to do about it.

Holly said with constraint, 'That's nice of them.'

She retrieved the discarded flute from the barman and began to dismantle it. Ramon watched.

'Is it damaged?'

She smiled. 'It's been through worse.' She stowed it carefully and snapped the flute case shut. 'You've been very kind. Thank you.'

She held her hand out. Ramon recognised finality. He took her hand with reluctance.

'I didn't do anything. You should be thanking Jack.'

'Both of you,' she conceded. 'I'm grateful. Really.'

She picked up the plastic bag and the flute case. Ramon thought of what Jack would say if she left like this. 'Aren't you staying here?'

'No.' She offered no further explanation.

Ramon's heart sank. 'I'm sure Jack was expecting...'

'Yes, we've discussed it. He knows I'm going home.'

She made for the door, undeterred. Ramon slip-stepped beside her.

'Won't you at least say goodbye to him?'

Holly sent him an ironic look. 'And disturb his work?'

'Well...'

He was so worried that Holly softened.

'You and Mr Armour have already given me more help than I have any right to expect from strangers,' she said kindly. 'Brendan is my problem and I must find a way to deal with him. This is where I start.'

'Gone!'

The receptionist was apologetic. 'I was off duty

when she left last night but…'

'Last night!' Jack swung round on Ramon. 'Did you know about this?'

Ramon thought he had never known Jack to lose his cool so completely. Under the smooth golden skin, he was white. A little muscle worked at his jaw.

Ramon shifted from one foot to the other. 'She said thank you,' he offered.

Jack's eyes narrowed. Ramon felt as if ice water was trickling down his spine. Then Jack turned away abruptly and reverted to the desk clerk. His mouth was tight as a vice.

'She must have left a message.'

The desk clerk scanned the pigeonholes.

Ramon twitched Jack's sleeve. 'I told you—she said thank you. And that you were working, so she didn't want to disturb you.'

Jack ignored him. There was a handful of messages. Some made Jack's eyebrows knit in a hard line. But, thought Ramon, reading his expression with an experienced eye, not one was what he was looking for. Ramon sighed.

'Nothing from Holly Dent, huh?'

'No.'

'So she's done a runner. Seems a habit with her. Well, at least that's one less thing for us to

worry about.' He just managed not to turn it into
a question.

Jack's face took on its stony look. Ramon had
seen that look before. He sighed; and decided that
he had to share last night's gossip after all.

'Look, Jack,' he said hardily, 'she was string-
ing us along. The guy who runs the club said she
was on the run from her husband.'

Jack just stared at him.

'In all likelihood, Brendan whatever-his-name-
was is her husband, not her brother-in-law,'
Ramon repeated urgently. 'You don't want to be
caught between husband and wife, do you?'

He did not add 'again'. He did not have to. The
dark, dark eyes looked at him as if they did not
see him.

'She was terrified,' Jack said almost to himself.

'She *said* she was terrified.' Ramon hesitated.
'Oh, what the hell? I looked in her flute case. The
name in it was not Holly Dent.'

That got a reaction all right. The dark eyes
lifted scorchingly.

'What was it?' Jack demanded. 'Sugrue?'

'N-no,' Ramon admitted, startled by the intensity. 'I don't remember. I didn't take much notice,
to be honest.'

'Too busy hustling her out of the door,' said
Jack, his mouth white.

Ramon was stung. 'That's not true. I told her you were expecting her to stay and she said you already knew she was leaving. All right, I was relieved. But I didn't persuade her. And I didn't hustle her out of the door.'

Jack riffled the papers between his fingers absently.

'I don't believe that girl is married,' he said at last.

Ramon flung up his hands. 'You don't *want* to believe.'

'Nonsense. Why should I care?'

'Exactly,' cried Ramon in triumph. 'Why do you care about a girl you never saw before yesterday?'

The papers stilled in Jack's hands.

'She was brave enough later but when she saw that man she went to pieces,' he said at last in a low voice. His mouth twisted as if he was in pain. 'No one should be that afraid.'

Ramon's heart sank. But he said robustly, 'When she went, she said Brendan was her problem and she would sort it out. She didn't want you interfering.'

There was a moment's silence. Then Jack gave a short laugh.

'The story of my life,' he said with savage self-mockery.

Ramon winced.

'It's OK, Ramon. You don't have to rub it in. I've got the message. Holly Dent doesn't need any help. I am off the hook.'

Ramon gave silent thanks.

Holly had a bad night, haunted by a tall man with high cheekbones and unreadable eyes. In the morning her tawny eyes were enormous in a face as pale as meringue. Even overworked Chef Pierre commented on it.

'You look rough,' he said helpfully. 'Did the boyfriend catch up with you after all?' He was Gilbert's cousin, which was how she had found the job at Club Thaïs in the first place.

Holly was tying an apron over her jeans. Her head reared up at that. 'He's no boyfriend of mine.'

Pierre did not stop filling quiches but his eyebrows flew up. 'You mean he really is your husband? I thought that story was just for Gilbert's benefit.'

'Oh,' she said understanding. 'You mean Brendan.'

This time Pierre did stop filling quiches. 'Who else?'

Holly flushed, appalled. Why on earth had her mind jumped to Jack Armour? She turned the tap

on and began to scrub her hands with quite unnecessary vigour.

'Never mind.'

He went back to his work. 'So which one
makes you look like only half of you came to
work this morning?'

Holly was startled. She peered at her wavery
reflection in the shiny steel draining board. 'That
bad?'

'Yes,' said Pierre brutally. 'So you got away
from Monsieur Brendan all right?'

She tensed involuntarily. Doing her best to ignore it, she pulled a face. 'So far.'

'I've warned the others. If the guy comes back
again they're not to tell him anything. They'll be
more careful next time.'

'Thanks,' said Holly.

But she was sure it would only be a matter of
time before Brendan tracked her down. He had
done it before—in Barcelona, in Dublin. No reason to think he would have lost his touch in Paris.
She would just have to leave as soon as possible.

She told Pierre as soon as they were alone in
the kitchen.

'I'm sorry. Of course I won't leave you in the
lurch. But I'd be really glad if you can get someone to take over from me before the end of the
week.'

The young chef's eyebrows rose. 'That soon? Going away with someone?'

Holly shook her head vigorously. 'Travelling alone. I always travel alone.'

But—just for a moment—she thought about Jack Armour again and wished...

Pierre laughed. And Holly, cheeks flaming, flung herself into rolling pastry with such energy that it ended up almost transparent.

The events of the night had left Jack in savage form, as the International Disaster Committee found to its cost. The Committee was willing to discuss detailed projections, said the Chair kindly. Now if they could just consider a few alternative scenarios...

Three hours later she was looking as if she had gone ten rounds with a world-class heavyweight. The coffee was long finished. Most of the bottles of mineral water were empty, too. And Jack was clearly just getting into his stride.

'Now, as you've already pointed out, Madam Chair, those last figures assume that all sites are accessible which, as we know, is not the case. So my next assumptions—'

He passed round a package of ten sheets or so, one for each person round the table. The committee's expressions ranged from horrified to de-

pressed. Ramon bit back a smile. Jack in negotiating mode was inventive.

'Well, perhaps we might take a short break,'
said the Chair desperately.

Jack managed to look disappointed. But he ac-
quiesced and soon they were out in the corridor
again.

'What are you doing?' muttered Ramon.
'Drowning them in paper?'

Jack's eyes glinted. 'Making a good case for
three times what we need. By the time I've finished with them, they'll think they were lucky to
settle for the base figure.'

He was right.

'I'll sign the letter of confirmation as soon as
the secretariat can prepare it,' said the Chair, giving in gracefully.

'Tonight,' the committee secretary assured her.

Jack frowned. 'But we need to start drawing
against the funds as soon as possible for the Ignaz
operation.'

'Don't worry, Mr Armour,' said the Chair, not
without a touch of malice. She knew that Jack
avoided official functions with skill and dedica-
tion. 'I've no doubt you'll be going to the
President's Dinner this evening. I'll have someone deliver it to you personally.'

For the second time that day, Ramon hid bubbling laughter.

The Place des Abbesses was one of the Métro's original stations. The stone steps came up to a lovely confection of curlicued iron railings at street level under a canopy of frosted glass. Normally Holly never emerged without taking a moment to savour that canopy. Its ribs of steel always reminded her of the pleats on an Edwardian bonnet.

Today she did not spare it a glance. Nor the trees in their lacy spring leaf. April sunshine blasted the white-painted buildings like a spotlight but Holly did not notice.

Where next? she was thinking. Brussels? London? But Brussels was too small. Brendan would find her even more easily than he had in Paris. And the thought of London appalled her, with its dirt and heartless crowds and, worst of all, its hurtful memories.

How was it that the memories of really good times could be more hurtful than pain?

She started back up the hill towards her rented room, brooding. How many more times could she pack up and move on? How much longer could she pretend that it did not matter that she had no home? That every time she made a friend she had to remind herself that the friendship was provisional until Brendan and all the Lansing family caught up with her again?

At least she had not pretended with Jack Armour, Holly thought suddenly. She had not had the time. Anyway, he had seen Brendan Sugrue at his bullying worst. So Jack Armour knew her as nobody else had done since she was a schoolgirl. It was an odd feeling. Scary but, somehow, a challenge…

Holly stopped dead, shocked. She was in front of a pillar advertising a new play and an old opera. She did not read either notice.

A challenge? *A challenge?* Was she seriously thinking that Gorgeous Jack and his high-handed ways would carry on strolling through her life? She had never met him before yesterday and he had hardly been conciliating. Surely she did not want to see the man again?

But he made me feel safe.

For a moment she almost thought she had spoken aloud. Holly was shocked. She looked round furtively. But none of the springtime tourists seemed to have heard anything. They went on chatting and photographing, hardly noticing as Holly pushed between them.

She took herself to task with force.

What sort of an idiot was she? Safety was a cruel illusion. The most you could hope for was peace of mind. All that men did was threaten that precarious equilibrium.

Well, maybe not all men. Some were like Chef Pierre, preoccupied but basically well-meaning. Some were carefully uninvolved, like Gilbert. And too many thought that they could sort out your problems by hijacking your life. You just could not afford to let them too close.

Remember Mum, thought Holly painfully. If ever there was a woman who had paid dearly for letting a man too close, it was her mother.

No, relying on yourself was best. It might get lonely sometimes. But loneliness was manageable. The sort of destruction sown by men like Brendan Sugrue and, Heaven help her, her tycoon father was not.

So she was going to stop dreaming wistful dreams about Jack Armour and make some sensible plans.

She set off briskly through the steep streets. She had a room over a café which boasted a romantic history of talented artists and impoverished musicians. The food was indifferent and the building horribly run down but the room was cheap and the landlord had not asked for references.

She smiled wryly. It was to be hoped that the next landlord in the next city would be equally relaxed. In the meantime, she had better pack her few possessions so that she could take off at a moment's notice.

She was just starting to do that when there was a perfunctory knock on the door of her room. Holly spun round, shocked into mouse stillness. Another knock—then the rickety door burst open as if someone had put his shoulder to it.

Holly stood frozen, her face perfectly white.

Jack Armour dusted off his hands, straightened his jacket and said, 'It's all right. It's me.'

Holly did not move.

With an impatient exclamation, he strode forward and put his hands on her shoulders. 'Don't look like that.'

Holly pulled herself together with a great effort. She twitched her shoulders out of his grasp.

'What are you doing here?' Her voice cracked.

He had been asking himself the very same thing, ever since he got her address from Gilbert at Le Club Thaïs. He had still not achieved an answer. So he ignored the question.

'We need to talk.'

'No, we don't.'

'Believe me, we do.'

Holly closed her eyes briefly. *He makes me feel safe*. That was crazy.

She opened her eyes. 'Why?' she said with an effort.

'Because Brendan Sugrue has been leaving messages for me,' he said levelly.

The sprinkling of freckles across her nose and cheekbones stood out like toast crumbs. With her long plait, she looked about six, Jack thought. It infuriated him. He wanted to take her face between his hands and tell her to trust him. That made him want to shout with rage. He did not.

Instead he half turned away and said in his most neutral voice, 'The hotel tells me he has been round in person twice already today.'

She looked sick. 'Oh, God.'

He waited.

At last she shook her head as if to clear it. 'What did you tell him?'

Jack's mouth thinned. 'Oh, sure, of course I told a violent man everything I knew about you. Which you had seen to wasn't much, for that matter. Good forward thinking, that.'

Holly realised she had angered him. 'I'm sorry. It's just that— How did he find the hotel? How did he know I'd been there?'

'The taxi cab from last night,' said Jack briefly. 'Brendan managed to track it down. I gather the driver told him where he had taken us and then the hotel confirmed that you'd been there. It never occurred to me to warn them not to.' He added thoughtfully, 'Say what you will, the man is resourceful.'

Holly's laugh grated. 'Oh, he's resourceful, all right.'

Jack watched her in silence for a moment. 'And is he your guardian? Or your husband?' His voice was so neutral now it could have come from a robot. 'Or something else entirely?'

Holly stared. 'What?'

'Your husband. Or maybe a discarded lover.'

Holly was so taken aback she laughed aloud. It brought some of the natural colour back into her cheeks, he saw. The skin was so soft. How would it feel to touch?

'You're joking, right?'

He wrenched his thoughts away from the image of a soft cheek caressing his palm and turned sternly to the matter in hand.

'He is very persistent. He seems to take your disappearance very personally.'

Her eyes flickered. 'He doesn't like to be crossed.'

Jack thought: She's lying. The beguiling image disappeared abruptly.

He said softly, 'Or he's in love with you.'

Holly shook her head fiercely. 'Brendan doesn't love anything but work.' She sounded desolate.

Jack held himself very still, scanning her expression. What made her look like that? Because she wanted the man to love her? It hadn't seemed like that yesterday, but...

She turned away. Jack watched her, his brows knitted.

'Were you in love with him? Did he let you down? Is that what this is all about?'

She swung back, her head high. 'I don't know what it's got to do with you—'

Jack interrupted. He said quietly, 'I got you out of there last night. That makes me involved.'

There was an odd silence. Jack's face was almost without expression. But there was something in his voice that brought Holly up short. She found that she was feeling breathless suddenly. She did not like it.

After a moment she said, 'Yeah, I suppose. But I'd have got myself out of it in the end.'

'Would you?'

'I have before.'

Jack nodded gravely. 'Like you were doing at the International Committee Building yesterday before I took a hand?'

She said heatedly, 'Are you trying to be unpleasant?'

A brief smile touched his mouth.

'Realistic,' he corrected.

Oh, that sexy mouth! She whipped her irritation back into life but it was an effort.

'Listen, I've been on my own since I was seventeen. I've done all right up to now.'

'It looks like it,' he agreed suavely.

She looked round at her few belongings. Half of them were tumbled on the bed. She saw it as he must see it and flushed.

'I know it's not the grandest room in the world,' she said defiantly. 'All right, compared with your hotel it's a bit of a slum. But this is a very historic area. I can have my Sunday morning brunch at a table where Apollinaire wrote and Utrillo painted.'

Jack blinked. 'Very cultural.' His voice quivered on a note of unexpected amusement. 'But you've got me wrong. I wasn't criticising your living arrangements.'

Holly glowered. 'What, then?'

He said gently, 'Forgive me, but I don't think you are dealing very successfully with Brendan Sugrue.'

'You know nothing about it.'

He strode forward, startling her, and picked up her half-packed roll bag.

'I know that running away doesn't solve anything.'

Holly stared at him incredulously. 'Put that down.'

'So you can finish packing and then run?' He shook his head. 'And then what? Another city? Another slum room? Another set of dead-end jobs?'

Holly glared. The man was not a mind-reader, she told herself. He was *not*.

'They pay the rent.'

'And keep you running.' He put the bag down and looked at her gravely. 'Can't you see that you have to face him and sort out whatever it is, once and for all?'

'I will. Just as soon as I'm twenty-five and they—I mean, he hasn't got a case any more.'

Jack shook his head. 'That's three years away.'

He remembered! Even in the middle of her anger and worry, Holly could not suppress a little thrill of triumph. She had told him almost nothing about herself, deliberately. Her age had slipped out when she was too panic-stricken to watch herself. And he had stored it away as if it were important information.

'You can't keep on the run for the next three years.'

'Watch me.'

He was odiously reasonable. 'Why put your life on hold for all that time? Look at this logically. You need to challenge that will. Or make a marriage of convenience.'

Holly could have danced with frustration. 'Yes, that would have got me off the hook all right. But back in Lansing Mills there was no one I could ask. And now...'

'Now you could ask me.'

There was a stunned silence. Holly pushed her fraying hair off her neck.

'Oh, sure,' she said with a brave attempt at flippancy. 'Just what I need. Marriage with the first man I can find, whether I trust him or not.'

Jack was dry. 'You mean there's a man in the world you might actually trust?'

Holly lost her flippancy.

'Marriage might work for the family,' she said shortly. 'Not for me. What's that thing about the cure being worse than the disease?'

She retrieved her bag. Plonking it on the bed, she began to stuff the contents of her bedside drawer into it. Her hands were not quite steady.

Jack watched that tell-tale shudder and set his teeth.

'So why would facing him be so bad?'

She stopped in her task for a moment. She did not look up but he saw her throat move as she swallowed convulsively.

'You're as tense as a spring,' he said involuntarily.

She paused, not looking at him, like a bird about to take wing. Jack tried another tack.

'Look,' he said, 'if you don't face him now, you will run away; he will follow; the whole cycle starts again. Where's the sense in that? Why don't you just sit round a table with him and work out a compromise?'

Still she did not look at him. Her face was bleak.

'Brendan doesn't compromise.'

He drew an impatient breath. 'I'd do it myself if I didn't have to get back to Ignaz.'

She looked up then. 'I told you, he doesn't listen. It wouldn't do any good. You or anyone else; it wouldn't change a thing. Brendan doesn't compromise.'

Jack ran his hands through his hair. 'This timing is the pits,' he muttered.

'What?'

'I just don't have time for this.'

It was almost as if he was talking to himself. But Holly had had enough. She rounded on him.

'Well, who asked you to vote, anyway? You haven't got time? Fine. Great. Why don't you just get lost?'

'And leave you alone to deal with the brother-in-law from hell?'

She paled, but she answered firmly enough. 'As you pointed out, I can run.'

'Oh, maybe you'll get away from him this time. Can't you see that's no answer?'

There was a commotion in the street. Jack looked out of the window.

'Correction. You're not getting away from him this time. Not unless this place has a fire escape.'

'What?' She rushed to the window. Climbing the hill below was a familiar thick-set figure. All the fight drained out of Holly. She went white to the lips and clung to the edge of the shutter.

'What *is* it about this guy?' said Jack exasperated.

Holly's lips felt numb. She shook her head, not answering.

Jack thought swiftly. 'OK. I'll get rid of him. Will you meet me at the hotel?'

She stared at him, blank. Then nodded jerkily, like a puppet.

He shook her gently. 'Not good enough. Will you go back to the hotel?' He fished in his inside pocket and brought out a wad of bills. 'Take a cab. OK?'

Holly swallowed. 'OK.'

'No running out on me?'

'All right.'

Still he hesitated. He put a hand gently under her chin and tipped her pale face up to meet his eyes.

'Still don't trust me?'

Her eyes fell.

'We'll just have to deal with that later. Meanwhile, no more taking off on your own. Promise?'

Holly blinked. 'I promise,' she said, surprised.

'Good. See you soon.'

He feathered a touch to her cheek before she could recoil. Then he turned and left. She heard him running lightly down the stairs and the front door opened and banged decisively shut.

From behind the shutter she peered down into the street and saw him and Brendan meet, argue and then Jack laugh mockingly. He turned and made off down the hill.

Brendan hesitated for a moment, clearly torn. Holly held her breath. But then Brendan turned on his heel and ran off down the hill after the man he must think would lead him to his quarry.

She flung the rest of things into the roll bag, picked up her flute case and ran. She forgot to look back.

So he'd got her into the room he had booked for her in the end, Holly thought. Late, maybe. But he'd got his own way. She resented that, when she recovered from her near-brush with Brendan and her brain was in working order again.

When he knocked on her door she was all set for battle.

But Jack was in severely practical mode. 'Not an attractive character, your brother-in-law,' he said, brushing past her. 'But I think I've held him off for the next few hours, at least.'

He sat down at the desk in the corner of the room and put his briefcase on the top. Holly was outraged at being ignored. Was he not even going to tell her what he had said to Brendan?

'What are you doing?' she demanded

Jack was surprised. 'Plugging in and logging on.'

He proceeded to do so. Holly saw that the case contained a small laptop computer.

'This is not your office,' she raged, obscurely offended.

'Outdated,' Jack said, mildly amused. 'No one has offices any more. Now—' He removed his attention for the screen and swung round on her while the little machine beeped and clicked industriously. 'Let's talk about the solutions to this problem of ours.'

'Mine,' said Holly with emphasis.

He waved that aside. 'Running doesn't work. You won't confront. It has to be marriage.'

'Thank you for that illuminating analysis, but—'

'Sarcasm,' said Jack calmly, 'does not become you. Now, marriage is not easy to achieve at the drop of a hat...' He looked back at the little screen.

Holly had a strong urge to throw things. At least that would get his attention off the laptop and back where it belonged.

'Marry *you*? I would rather—'

He swung round neatly and looked her straight in the eyes.

'Face Brendan Sugrue?'

She was silenced.

'No, I thought not.' He went back to his computer. 'Now, I admit that marriage without trust is a real bummer. Under ordinary circumstances I wouldn't consider it. So—'

Like a magician he whisked a couple of sheets of paper from a pocket in the back of the briefcase. He handed them out towards her, not taking his eyes off the screen.

To her fury, Holly found herself taking them. 'What's this?'

'My CV.'

'What?'

'The story of my life,' said Jack ironically.

'What am I supposed to do with it?'

'Try reading.'

The machine beeped an imperious note. He leaned forward and typed a spray of instructions.

Over his shoulder he said, 'You don't trust me partly because you don't know me. Well, there I am. But first, give me your passport.'

'What?'

He snapped his fingers. 'Passport. I'm checking some options.'

For a moment Holly was mutinous. 'Why should I?'

'Because they are your options, not mine,' said Jack with the sort of careful patience that made her want to hit him. He scooted the chair back from the desk and looked up at her mockingly. 'But if you'd rather surf the net yourself, be my guest.' And he gestured at the laptop.

Holly gave him the passport in furious silence.

He flicked through it, filled in a couple of boxes on the computer screen and said casually, 'An

English passport? I thought you were from Smallville, USA?'

'My mother was English,' said Holly curtly. 'I was brought up there until I was fifteen.'

'Ah.' He answered a question from the computer. 'And I suppose that's why the passport says you're Holly Anne Dent but the plate in your flute case says you're Holly Lansing?'

Yes, that had been a mistake. She was still cursing her carelessness when Jack swung round on her. He was so fast that Holly had no time for disguise. So there was no way she could hide her consternation, she thought. Still, she always thought best on her feet.

'Lansing is my stage name,' she said defiantly. 'Musicians all have a stage name here in Paris.'

His eyes narrowed to slits. There was a silence that twanged like a bowstring. Then he gave a short laugh and turned back to his screen.

'Good recovery,' he told her. But he did not say that he believed her.

Of course, international know-it-all that he was, he probably realised she was talking nonsense. Just as long as he didn't make the connection to Lansing Industries, she did not care what he thought of her.

This man was all that stood between her and Brendan's plans for her unless she was very careful. She could not afford for him to deduce that she was heir to half the Lansing millions. Not when she had overheard Jack telling Ramon that what their company needed was a friendly millionaire. Brendan would be very friendly to someone who told him where the missing heiress was.

So she shrugged and made a great business about transferring her attention to the closely typed sheets he had given her.

'''US national. Born Manila. Unmarried, no children. Princeton, Cambridge, Osaka'',' she read aloud. '''Blah, blah, Smart Buildings Inc. World Bank project, blah, blah. Principal shareholder and CEO Armour Disaster Recovery, based in Delaware, subsidiary companies Miami, Florida, Nagoya, Japan, Shropshire, England. Publications, blah, blah. e-mail address, blah. Permanent residence…''' She looked up. 'That's blank. You don't live anywhere?'

A faint look of annoyance creased the handsome face.

'Trust you to pick out the one hole in my seamless history.' He was not as amused as he was trying to sound, Holly thought. 'I pretty much live on the road. My office in Miami can always find me.'

'But no home at all?'

He thumped the keyboard twice with quite unnecessary vigour.

'I bought a house in England years ago. I've still got it. I don't often go there.'

'Why?'

He glared at the screen. 'I should never have bought it. Sheer romanticism. It was crazy. Investment in real estate is not my forte.'

Holly did not understand and it was clear that Jack was not going to enlighten her.

She said, 'So your family don't live in England?'

'My family live all over the world,' he said uncommunicatively.

'I mean your parents. Brothers and sisters.'

He did not look away from the screen. Without apparent interest, he said, 'Parents dead. No siblings.'

The lack of feeling would have been chilling if she had not had a sudden, inexplicable sense again of that inflammable mixture seething away below the surface.

'So where was your home when you were a child?' she probed cautiously.

He nodded at the paper in her hand before going back to the computer. 'My dad was in the military. My parents divorced when I was eight. After that I shuttled between them until she died.

He was posted. I went back to the States to school, then on to college. I never lived with him after I was sixteen. I never lived with anybody.'

So that explained his air of containment. Holly felt a sneaking sympathy. She suppressed it. Jack Armour didn't need her sympathy or anyone else's and she had to keep her wits about her. He might make her feel safe but that could so easily turn into an emotional trap. She could not afford that.

So she said in a hard voice, 'So you're the man from nowhere? And I'm supposed to trust you?'

He turned away from the computer.

'Forget the blanks. Concentrate on what I've done. That ought to tell you something about me.'

She shook the papers. 'This is supposed to mean something to me? I've heard of the World Bank but that's about it. Is there really a company called Smart Buildings?'

Jack smiled. 'Smart buildings learn and adapt. Cutting edge of technology. I did a lot of research in that area until I realised that we could use the technology we had a hell of a lot better than we do. That's when I set up Armour Disaster Recovery.'

'You're a scientist,' she said on a note of discovery.

He frowned. 'I'm a problem-solver.'

Holly raised her brows. 'And I'm a problem to be solved?'

'You have a problem that needs solving,' he corrected. 'And soon.'

She ground her teeth. 'And you think you're the man to do it?'

'I know I am,' said Jack superbly. 'I have the experience. I have the vision. And I'm not emotionally involved.'

'Great,' said Holly under her breath. 'Just what I need. A professional busybody.'

Jack glared. The computer beeped again. For the first time he ignored it.

'Look,' he said, getting to his feet, 'I'm willing to help but don't push me.'

Holly stared, affronted. He ran an impatient hand through his hair.

'I know you don't trust easily,' he said in level voice. 'OK. I accept that. I even accept that you need to know something about me before you take my advice.'

'Advice? Huh! Orders, more like.'

He ignored that. 'You may not recognise the names on my CV but believe me they are the great and the good in the disaster relief world. Now, this evening Ramon and I have to go to a reception where a fair number of them will be. So the practical solution is for you to come too.'

Holly could hardly believe her ears. 'You want me to go out with you?'

Jack looked down his nose. 'Not on a date. This is strictly business from my point of view. You can use it to—er—take up my references.'

Holly glared at him, searching about in her mind for the most blistering thing she could think of to tell him exactly what she thought of his practical solutions.

In the end, and to her dismay, all she came up with was a heartfelt cry, 'What will I *wear*?'

Jack was supremely uninterested. 'Nothing grand. Business suit will do.'

In spite of herself, Holly gave a choke of laughter. 'Like I have a business suit!'

He had the grace to look uncomfortable. 'No, of course not. Well—'

'I can do a little black dress,' she offered.

'Show me.'

She did. It was cheap stretchy satin, long-sleeved and short-skirted. Holly surveyed it ruefully.

'I bought it when I got a job playing in a band. Dublin, that was. It scrunches up to nothing but the creases just fall out when you shake it.'

She demonstrated.

Jack nodded. 'It'll do.'

It did more than that. When he and Ramon were waiting in their tuxedos, he did not recognise the poised woman who walked into the hotel lobby. Golden-brown hair was piled into a loose coronet, revealing a graceful neck and a spectacular cascade of multi-coloured earrings. The crease-resistant dress clung.

'Yes!' said Ramon in purely masculine appreciation.

Jack did a double-take. This was no teenage scruff in a bargain-basement dress. This was total confidence.

For some reason, it shook him. He had seen Holly Dent, Lansing, or whatever her name was, as variously combative, truculent and terrified. On every occasion he had been struck by her vulnerability, her youth. The sexy siren was a revelation. Not, he found, a welcome one.

He did not admit it. He went through the whole evening on a sort of frozen courtesy that intimidated hosts and other guests alike. The only person it seemed to have no effect on was Holly Dent.

'Aren't you ever pleasant to people?' she said, after he had speared a persistent editor with an icy put-down. 'The man was only doing his job.'

Jack shrugged. 'It's not important.'

'Well, pardon me for breathing,' said Holly, outraged.

Jack stopped dead in his tracks. 'That guy,' he told her, 'is a waste of my time.'

'And I thought you believed in the brotherhood of man,' she mocked.

'Man, maybe,' said Jack unwarily. 'Let a woman loose with a camera and the world goes mad.'

Holly was confused. 'What woman?'

He was regretting letting that out. 'Oh, just some photographer who turned up at the current site. She works for him.'

'And you don't like her because she's a woman?' Holly shook her head. 'Your prejudices are showing.'

'I like her fine. I don't like her cute ideas.'

Holly grinned. 'Woman shouldn't have ideas, right? Anyone ever told you you're a dinosaur?'

'No.'

'Then they should have.'

'Not because I don't want to do a fashion shoot!' said Jack, goaded.

Holly blinked. 'Fashion? A fashion shoot?' She did not believe it. She started again. 'This photographer wanted you to be a sort of male model?' she said gropingly.

Jack was scanning the room again. 'Yes.'

'Fashion in what, for heaven's sake? Civil servant chic?'

That made him look at her. Jack stared in the blankest astonishment.

'What?'

Not pleased, thought Holly with quiet satisfaction. A glass of white port had given her a slight pounding in the temples and an agreeable sense of irresponsibility. Not pleased at all; what would happen if she wound the screw tighter?

'Well, that's what you do, isn't it?' She made a large gesture which spilt some of the wine on the velvety carpet. 'I've been checking your CV, like you told me. It sounds to me as if what you do is write papers for committees and go to meetings.' It was clear that she was not impressed.

There was an incredulous silence.

'I put up emergency housing after natural disasters,' Jack said at last. His voice was clipped. 'Meetings are the price I pay for the funding.'

'Oh. Sorry.' But she did not sound it and she knew it.

He shrugged again. 'No need to apologise.'

She took his arm. It was meant to be placating. It did not have the desired effect.

Jack froze. And Holly, after a startled double-take, withdrew her hand with a laugh that was too bright and altogether unconvincing.

'Why are you glowering?' she said, trying to make a joke of it and not quite succeeding.

He looked at her with dislike. 'I am not glowering.'

'Are, too.' She sipped the port, laughing at him over the top of the glass.

She must have been a better actress than she thought. Jack seemed convinced. At least, he did not point out that her laughter was hollow.

'Are you always this irritating?' he asked in a goaded voice.

Holly chuckled with real amusement at that. Irritating was better than horribly self-conscious any day of the week. 'I try.'

'Then I'm astonished your family want you back.'

As soon as he said it, he wished it unsaid. Even before the light died in the lively little face. He saw memory come back and could have kicked himself.

'I shouldn't have said that. My turn to apologise.'

There was a tiny pause.

'Don't worry about it.'

But she was subdued for the rest of the evening. When they got back to the hotel she refused to go into the bar with the two men and left them with a monosyllabic goodnight.

'Damn,' muttered Jack under his breath.

Ramon ordered a couple of brandies and they took them to a table under a parlour palm. The bar was still half full.

Ramon got straight to the point. 'What are you going to do about her?'

'What can I do? The obvious solution is for her to marry me.'

Ramon wisely did not comment.

Jack shifted irritably. 'She just can't make up her mind if she wants my help or not.'

'What sort of help are you offering?' Ramon asked practically. 'If marriage is off, I mean?'

Jack shifted his shoulders irritably. 'I haven't thought. A job, perhaps. Contacts, people who will find her a place to stay and something to do. Maybe even legal advice. I don't really understand how—'

'Look out,' said Ramon. 'Here she is.'

She was threading her way through the tables. As she got to them, they saw that her face was perfectly white. Jack surged to his feet.

'What's wrong?'

'Brendan,' she said, as soon as she got to them. 'He was here. *Here*.'

She thrust a paper towards Jack. Her hand was shaking so much that the little message fluttered like a fan. Jack twitched it out of her fingers and stuffed it in his pocket. He put an arm round her shoulders, sending a casual look round the room.

'I don't see him.'

'He's coming back,' said Holly. She looked sick.

Jack urged her to the door. 'Then let's get out of here. Coming, Ramon?'

They went to her room. Jack steered her into a seat and cast a quick eye down the black scrawled message. Brendan did indeed say he would be back, bringing legal reinforcements.

He sat down, regarding her with frowning concern.

'This is France. He'll find he can't just kidnap a person of your age against her will.'

Her hand lay on a little occasional table. The charms on her bracelet rattled against the wooden surface as she trembled. Jack put a strong hand over hers.

'You're your own person. You can deal with him,' he said, suddenly calm and not dictatorial at all.

Ramon said, 'He's right.'

She swallowed. 'I can't.'

'We'll be with you.'

'You don't understand. I *can't*.'

Jack did not waste time arguing. 'Then I'll get you a lawyer—'

'I've tried that.' Her mouth was shaking. 'The only guaranteed way to get away from the family is marriage. Anything else—' Her voice shook. 'It could stay in the courts for months and in the meantime he would have the right to—to—'

'Why are you so afraid of him?' Jack demanded softly. 'You're not afraid of anyone else.'

Both the men were staring at her as if she were a specimen in a laboratory. And she was too out of control even to resent it! Holly shut her eyes.

'He drowns me.'

There was an incredulous silence. Even with her eyes shut she could feel the two men looking at each other. Despising her.

Jack said in the infuriatingly reasonable tone of his, 'Then marry someone who doesn't drown you, if that's what it takes. And stop running away.'

Holly's eyes snapped open. The trembling increased.

'You mean, marry you.'

Their eyes locked. A muscle worked in his jaw.

'If that's what it takes.'

Five years of making her own way and avoiding situations she knew she could not handle screamed at Holly to say no. Perhaps if he had not suddenly turned away she would have done. Perhaps if he had not released her from that commanding gaze she would have done. Perhaps if he had not found her jacket and put it so carefully round her shoulders…

'It's all right,' he said softly. 'You don't have to do anything you don't want to.'

He held the denim round her like a comforting cloak. The trembling changed.

Say no! Say no!

'Yes,' she said.

CHAPTER FOUR

IT WAS all so easy after that. Crazily easy, in Holly's opinion. Surely it shouldn't be that easy to throw away your life on an unthought-out impulse? She even said so to Jack as they sat opposite each other on the train going under the English Channel.

He shrugged. 'What do you expect?'

'But marriage.' She shivered superstitiously. 'There should be more—hurdles.'

He laughed and leaned towards her. For a moment Holly thought he was going to touch her. She held her breath, wanting it, not wanting it, not knowing...

But he had seen the way she tensed. His face hardened.

'You want someone to forbid the banns? Brendan Sugrue, maybe?'

Holly flinched 'No, of course not.'

'Do it or don't do it. But take responsibility for your own choices, for God's sake.'

'I do.' She straightened indignantly, forgetting her superstitions. 'I always have done.'

'Then stop cowering and tell me what sort of ring you want.'

'I don't cower,' said Holly disgusted. 'I merely—' Her ears caught up with her. 'Ring? What ring?'

'If you turn up in Sugar Island without a ring, no one will believe you're engaged to me,' said Jack.

Sugar Island was where they were going to be married. Her heart lurched at the thought.

She found he was looking her up and down deliberately. He did not say *No one will believe it anyway*. Holly felt her colour rise.

'Does it matter what they believe?' she demanded, belligerent to hide her confusion.

'I've sworn a declaration for both of us. If we don't look like a conventional couple, people will start asking questions,' he pointed out.

Holly glared at him for an impotent moment. Then she gave a husky laugh as if it was punched out of her.

'I loathe you when you're being reasonable.'

'That figures,' said Jack, smiling.

Was it the too bright light as the train went through the tunnel or did the smile really not reach his eyes?

In London he took her to a magician's cave of jewels in a back alley. Holly was too intimidated by all the mineral glitter on show to offer an opinion. In the end Jack pointed impatiently to a large diamond.

'Go with the dinosaur's choice,' he said to her with faint acidity.

Holly tried not to show her reluctance as he slid it onto her finger. The ring felt as heavy as handcuffs. And the pulse in his wrist against her own felt like a steam hammer. Startled, she looked up.

But Jack did not notice. Or did not want to notice. He was already turning away, bringing out his credit card, ignoring her. Again.

Jack, Holly thought, concentrated all his attention on one thing at a time. Usually it was not her. Part of her was grateful for that, of course. But part of her was piqued that he found it so easy to ignore her.

She said so.

He was setting a brisk pace down a narrow street but at that he stopped and looked down at her. The strange eyes narrowed to slits.

'You want me to concentrate on you?'

Holly felt as if someone had inserted an icicle down the neck of her shirt and she had only just realised it.

'I didn't say that.'

'That's what you meant.'

'No, I—'

'As it happens, I agree with you.' He started walking again. But he did not take his eyes off her disturbed face. 'We're overdue a long talk. For instance—when did Miss Lansing turn into Miss Dent?'

That damned flute case! She should have known that he would not believe her story about a stage name. Silently Holly damned her own carelessness and sought for an answer he would believe.

'Was it, for example, when you left Smallville, USA?'

She glared.

'It's not so hard to work out,' he told her, amused. 'But that passport is genuine. I checked.'

Her heart did a somersault. 'You've been checking up on me?'

'I swore a legal oath that you were free to marry me,' he reminded her softly. 'Of course I checked.'

She reminded herself that she had never actually told him a lie.

'So are you satisfied?'

His eyes narrowed to slits. 'I think you already know the answer to that.'

She felt challenge roll out at her like a huge wave. It was not his tone, nor the way he looked at her. It was the way he stood, impatience barely curbed; and the ring on her finger. Oh, help, thought Holly. Her heart began to race. Oh, *help*.

And then he let her off the hook. 'But we can talk about it later. Now we have to find you a room for the night.'

He did that, as he did everything else, with minimum fuss, maximum efficiency and absolutely no consultation of her wishes at all. It was like being caught up in a tornado. You were whirled round at a hundred times your normal speed, while he just surged on. He never broke into a sweat and he was absolutely unstoppable.

And unreadable. Holly just had no idea what he was thinking, ever. Even when he took her to his house on the edge of the Welsh Marches and it turned out to be a castle, he was still as much of a stranger as he had ever been. She went through the ancient house while he worked in his study and she did not find so much as a book or an old photograph to give her a clue about who he really was.

When he said goodbye to her at Gatwick Airport, Holly felt lightheaded with the sheer strangeness of it all. She knew nothing more about him than she had after reading his CV. He seemed to want to hide himself from her deliberately.

Was she crazy, marrying him?

She was still asking herself that as she stood outside the luxurious cabin he had booked for her, with the sounds of the Caribbean night filling her skittering mind. Her loosened hair wafted about her bare shoulders in a sham caress. She shivered. She had never felt so alone.

Two days' residence on Sugar Island and she was qualified to marry Jack in an island ceremony. Jack had arranged it all, even down to employing Paula Vincent to take charge of the arrangements until he arrived on the island.

Half the time Holly felt as if she was caught up in a dream. No one had ever made her feel as safe as Jack had in that moment when he put that jacket round her. And no one had ever made her feel so insecure.

Which brought her here, alone under strange and brilliant stars, suddenly realising that she had reached a turning point in her life. Footloose and free was never going to be quite enough again.

'And I thought I knew all the ways there were to be frightened,' Holly said aloud.

Paula Vincent stuck her head out of the French windows that led into the cabin.

'Sorry?'

Holly jumped. However alone she felt, Paula had met her off the plane and stuck to her side like a bodyguard ever since.

'Nothing. Just talking to myself,' Holly admitted with a grimace.

Paula nodded. Her dark eyes were kind. 'Who can blame you? But there's really no need to worry.'

'Isn't there?'

Holly rubbed her chilly arms. Paula looked remorseful.

'I'll get you a shawl. That dress was never designed for a wedding at midnight. Sorry!'

She disappeared into the cabin.

Holly's smile was twisted. Paula was right to claim responsibility. If it were not for Paula Vincent, Sugar Island's own wedding consultant, Holly would not be standing here bare-shouldered, with soft cream skirts stirring gently about her ankles. She would be in her habitual trousers and T-shirt. Maybe she would have added a smart-but-casual jacket that she had bought to get her through interviews and airport arrival lounges. Until today she had not worn a long dress in years.

A sea-scented breeze curled up the slopes of sugar cane from the beach. Palm leaves rattled. Cicadas sawed. And beyond, steady as the pulse of the world, there was the beat of the surf on the unseen beach.

'A night for love,' said Holly aloud. For all her intended cynicism she sounded young and breathless, even to her own ears. She tried again, 'Passion under a tropical sky…'

Her hands clenched on the balustrade. The grip was so tight that the wood scored her palm. The new diamond ring cut into her. She looked down at it.

She had taken it off, the first day. It was too valuable, she'd said. She was not used to it. She might lose it…

But Jack had been implacable. 'We're not talking Aladdin's treasure here.' He extracted the ring from the velvet nest to which she had restored it and held out his hand.

Holly went into full retreat. She put her hands under the table. She knew he must think she was behaving like a stubborn child and she couldn't do a thing about it.

'I'm in your debt enough.'

His amusement died. 'I've told you. It's not a gift, it's part of the disguise,' he said curtly. 'If you want people to accept the story you've got to play the part.'

For a moment his eyes bored into hers. Holly said nothing. Jack snapped the box shut and put it down on the table between them.

'Up to you,' he said softly.

So she wore it. Not, in the end, because her disguise demanded it. Because she wanted to.

It worried her. It felt as if she was breaching one of her mother's cardinal rules: putting herself in the power of one of those creatures who could break your heart.

Except that Jack couldn't break my heart. You have to love someone for them to be able to hurt you. I don't love Jack. Thank God.

Paula came out of the cabin with a shawl in one hand and a softly burring mobile phone in the other. She tossed the bright fringed stuff to Holly and answered. 'Hi. That you, Bob?'

Holly pulled the shawl round her. It was exquisitely soft but its touch did not seem to warm her skin at all. Paula did not notice; she was too busy listening. A frown gathered between her brows.

She said impatiently. 'So you keep the airport open until the man arrives.'

The mobile phone squawked.

Paula was having no truck with excuses. 'Just tell him ''hurricane''. Remind him what Jack Armour did for us.' She gave Holly a sudden wicked grin. 'If that fails, ask him if he wants Sugar Island to have a tourist industry or not.'

A pause. For no reason she could think of, Holly held her breath.

'This is the guy's wedding, for heaven's sake. You want to break's the bride's heart?'

Holly flinched.

'Great headline that would make,' said Paula, not noticing. She lowered the mobile phone. 'You want to tell him something? Message for Jack, maybe?'

Holly panicked. *'No!'*

Paula misinterpreted. Or maybe she chose to misinterpret. She went back to the attack.

'I've got a bride falling apart here,' she told her interlocutor forcefully. 'You get the man on the island and up here to his wedding. Or I'll make sure everyone knows who got in the way.'

She snapped the phone shut.

'That Bob is an idiot. They should never have given him a uniform. It's got him thinking he rules the world.' She looked at Holly narrowly. 'You're not really upset, are you, honey?'

Holly shook her head. The movement made her long loose curls fly. Another tribute to Paula's powers of persuasion.

'You can't go to your wedding with your hair in plaits,' she had said, genuinely shocked.

So Holly had washed her hair and combed it out until it fell into a waterfall of golden-brown pre-Raphaelite waves which satisfied Paula. Holly, facing an image in the mirror that she had never seen before, had gone into shock. She had never looked so pretty. So—she'd swallowed— *feminine*.

Now Paula said comfortingly, 'Jack will get here. Never known him to give up if something is important. Jack always keeps his promises.'

'You must know him very well.' Holly sounded strangled.

Paula thought she knew why. 'Hey, I'm a respectable married woman. I love the guy like a brother, that's all.'

She thinks I'm jealous, thought Holly. She said abruptly, 'I'm really cold. I need a coat.'

She went back into the cabin and grabbed her old denim jacket. It was battered and not very clean but it would protect her a bit.

She pulled it round her shoulders, remembering Paris and a man putting this same jacket around her while she shook. Not from cold then. Holly caught the jacket collar to her face and rubbed her cheek against it. Was it her imagination, or did it still smell of him? Yes, it was there: elusive as smoke, faint as a whisper in the dark, disturbing as a dream.

How could I be jealous? I know nothing about him, she thought. *Nothing. What am I doing here?*

But it was too late to ask that. She was here and, what was more, she had given Jack her word. She always kept her word. In the terrible mess of her teenage years, that was the one truth she had held on to. From what Paula said, it seemed it was one she shared with Jack.

She went back onto the verandah, hoping Paula would ascribe her pallor to the temperature. She pulled the familiar jacket closer, with a theatrical murmur of appreciation. 'That's better.'

Paula did not seem to be deceived. She surveyed Holly critically. 'Hey. No need to look like that.'

'Like what?' said Holly, trying not to bristle.

'Like you've got to climb Everest. Everything's taken care of. Organising weddings is my business.'

'I'm sorry. The waiting must be getting to me.'

Paula nodded understandingly. 'Any bride would be upset.'

Holly flinched again. There was that word, for the second time tonight. Any bride.

Paula did not notice. 'Sugar Islanders are used to planes arriving late. We know it's not worth getting steamed up about. It's different for you.'

Any *bride*, thought Holly, almost with horror.

'Jack will be here. Bob says he's found a pilot to fly him in from Barbados. They'll keep the airport open here until he lands.'

Her conversation with the distant Bob suddenly fell into place.

'Thanks to you,' said Holly, enlightened.

Paula shrugged. 'Thanks to Jack. I just reminded Bob.'

'Reminded him?'

Paula's eyes narrowed. 'Didn't Jack tell you? We had a hurricane here a couple of years ago. Jack was on the relief team.'

'I know his company makes emergency housing…'

'Yeah, sure. His company made tents and stuff. But Jack was *here*. Mucking in with us. He didn't go until everyone had a roof over their heads again, even if it was only canvas.'

Holly had a vision of Jack, analysing the problem, working it out. And then he would tell everybody what to do. Calmly, logically and with no hint of emotion—and making quite sure that they did exactly what he said.

'Sounds like Jack.'

'He's got a lot of friends on Sugar Island after that.'

Holly looked away. They knew him, really knew him. She did not. They trusted him, admired him. Surely she could take comfort from that?

Yet when she thought about him, Jack was as alien as the moon. Jack of the slanting dark eyes; Jack of the disconcerting silences; Jack who was still and deep as a mountain lake and whom she did not begin to know. Whom she was going to make vows to tonight that neither he nor she meant. Who, she now realised, had not given her one good reason why he was so determined to marry her.

Holly tipped her head back and stared at the stars. She felt cold to her bones. But it did not have much to do with the increasing chill of the tropic night. Though she had done her best to hide it from herself, it was a cold that had started in Paris.

He can't hurt me. I'm not in love with him.

And then, slow as a building wave, *Am I?*

Stop, she told herself. *Ask yourself the basics. Has he made a pass? No.*

She had repelled enough passes to be sure of that.

Has he suggested he's attracted to you? No. Do you want him to? No.

She began to feel better. Also slightly ashamed of herself.

Hell, he hasn't even kissed me properly. What on earth am I getting myself into this state for?

Meanwhile Paula's phone was ringing again. Holly jumped, brought back to the present with a bump.

'Hello? Hi, Vinny. How you doing?'

Holly could hear the other end of the conversation. Great news: the little Islander had landed. Yes, they had processed Jack's passport and customs clearance while he was getting changed in the rest room. The whole party would be at Haven Beach in half an hour.

'Right, we're rolling,' said Paula. She gave Holly a grin. 'You can stop worrying. You're not going to be jilted at the altar.'

Holly tried to respond in kind. She really did.

'That's a relief.' She stood up.

Paula, confronted by a self-contained woman with frighteningly blank eyes, thought she had never seen a bride look like that. She tried hard to put it down to bridal nerves. She liked Jack Armour.

She tried to be encouraging. 'Want a last drink as a free woman?'

Free? Holly shuddered at all the implications of that. Then she took herself to task.

This was a marriage of convenience, pure and simple. They both knew that, she and Jack. She had no reason to think he had any intention to lock her into anything she didn't want. Unlike Homer Whittard, he had no ulterior motive for marrying her. Jack Armour was just a practical man with a strong protective streak who had decided that she was making a terrible job of solving her own problems. She sometimes thought that he had taken her future into his own hands out of pure impatience.

So why did he make her feel so insecure?

Because she was not used to being taken care of, Holly assured herself. She did not know how to respond. But she was really lucky that he was that sort of man.

Yes, that was the idea to cling on to. He was chivalrous. She was lucky. There was no need for her to feel as if she were about to jump off a cliff. Everything was going to work out *fine*.

'Here,' said Paula. She put a glass into Holly's hand. 'Fruit juice cocktail,' she explained. 'You want a dash of rum to stoke the fire?'

For a heartbeat, Holly turned to stone. All the things Paula thought she was feeling—all the things a normal bride would be feeling—surged up into a tidal wave and knocked the breath out of her. Then she took hold of herself. She shook her head violently.

'How long have I got?' Her voice sounded strange to her own ears but at least it was steady.

'Depends on how long you want to keep him waiting.'

Her throat nearly closed again. Holly worked hard on keeping her expression blank and breathed through it.

Paula Vincent sighed. She had hoped a little joke would lighten the atmosphere. Wrong, obviously!

She refused to be downcast. 'OK,' she said brightly. 'This is your last chance to freshen up as a single woman. Grab it. And I'll tell Proteus to bring the car round.'

Proteus turned out to be the taxi-driver who had met her at the airport. He was also the hotel barman and all-purpose wedding witness. The car was a flower-decked beach buggy which bounced to a halt on the grass below Holly's verandah.

'You go with Proteus in about ten minutes,' Paula told her. 'I'll get on down to the beach.' She gave her a quick, embarrassed kiss. 'Good luck. See you at the party.'

She went.

Proteus strolled up the steps. 'Shame you missed sunset. But you got a great night for it.'

Holly nodded. She grabbed at the chance of a neutral conversation. Her heart was thudding somewhere up in her throat and her spine kept giving little shudders. Adrenaline, she told herself. That was what it was. Not foreboding. Certainly not panic. Adrenaline and all perfectly normal. She was still grateful to discuss local marriage customs instead of how Gorgeous Jack always kept his promises.

She cleared her throat. 'Is that when people usually get married, then? Sunset?'

Proteus flashed a white grin in the darkness.

'Depends. They want a pretty sky for the photographs. Sunrise for the romantics. They want to be alone. Sunset for the ones who want to party.'

Holly was amused in spite of herself. 'Makes sense,' she said gravely.

'And Jack was always going to have a hell of a party.'

Holly was taken aback. As far as she knew Jack had decided they would marry on Sugar Island entirely because the official papers would take too long to organise in France—or in England, where her passport had been issued, or Florida, where his company was based. Yet here was Proteus talking as if Sugar Island was Jack's home and his local friends had always expected to dance at his wedding.

The sensation of being on a runaway dream ride struck her again.

'W-was he?'

Proteus smiled reminiscently. 'He was here after the hurricane. Brought those dinky little tents of his, all done up in cookie packets.'

'I see,' said Holly enlightened. 'Paula told me that he had done good work here. But I didn't realise you were so close to him.'

'Jack and me and Roy Vincent, we all put together the emergency generator at this end of the island. The guys and I promised him then—bring your lady on a trip when the island is back on its feet. And then Paula said, ''Get married here and we'll give you the best beach front wedding you've ever heard of.'''

'I see,' Holly said again, faintly.

It had not occurred to her that Jack might already have a girlfriend he wanted to marry. *Why* had it not occurred to her? A sexy man like that? Of course he would have a girlfriend.

So where was she? Why had he not married her, after all? And why was he willing to marry Holly, as if it did not matter who he married?

'So Paula was half expecting it when he called,' she said, fishing.

'Hell, no. Expecting it? When do you ever expect Jack Armour to do anything? He blows in when he feels like it. She was pleased, though. We all were.'

Great, thought Holly. *Just what I need. A wedding full of guests who know the groom better than I do.*

And then a small voice said in her ear, *Anyone who's ever met him knows him better than you do.*

She said curiously, 'Is it true they kept the airport open specially for him tonight?'

'Sure.'

'Just because his company built you some shelter after the hurricane?' She was incredulous.

Just like Paula, he was indignant at the suggestion that Jack had been doing no more than his job.

'Hey, not so much of the company talk. The man was hauling people out of buildings along with the rest of us. He got friends here. The guys will check his plane, then they'll all come on down to the beach for a few hours. Drink your health. Dance a while.'

Holly was beginning to be alarmed. 'It sounds like a major production.'

Proteus looked at her in surprise. 'No production. Just friends and food and some good music.'

Holly had a sudden memory of the party she had fled five years before. The Lansing Mills house had been full of formal flower arrangements and the garden full of circling waiters.

Donna had spent months in detailed preparations, including countless phone calls to brief the tuxedoed band. Holly could not imagine a party being organised in that house at a week's notice.

Involuntarily she smiled.

Proteus beamed back. 'It will be real pleasure to give you a good send-off,' he said. 'Jack said you had a lot of responsibilities. Didn't say how young you were, though.'

Clearly it was a cause for congratulation. Holly shifted uncomfortably.

'I don't think—'

'When I first saw you, I thought Jack had got him a schoolgirl,' he admitted.

Proteus had driven her from the airport.

'I hate flying. It always shows.' Holly was impatient. She wanted to know more about what Jack had told these people. She had a strong suspicion that he must have been talking about another woman altogether. 'When did Jack—?'

'No, wasn't jet-lag. Maybe it was your hair. Don't see a lot of grown-up ladies with plaits on Sugar Island.' He eyed her current tumble of brown-gold curls with approval. 'That's better.'

But Holly did not smile. 'When did Jack tell you I had a lot of responsibilities?'

He was apologetic. 'When you take a break, guys like to talk about normal stuff.'

'Take a break? You mean when he was here? After the hurricane?'

'Yes.'

So the unknown girlfriend had a lot of responsibilities. And after the hurricane Jack had expected to marry her. So why hadn't he?

And, more important, why was he marrying Holly? *Why?*

Proteus was alarmed by her silence. 'Wasn't anything—you know—private,' he assured her. 'Guys don't talk secrets like women do.'

She pulled herself together. 'It doesn't matter. How soon should we go?'

'Soon as you like. Jack should be there by now.'

The verandah lurched under her feet.

'Oh.' She put a hand to her throat. 'I think I feel sick.'

Proteus grinned, unperturbed. 'Never knew a bride yet who didn't have wedding nerves. You'll be OK soon as you see Jack.'

There was that word again. *Bride.* The trouble was, she was beginning to believe it. Holly repressed a desire to moan.

'Will I?'

'Or when the party gets going.'

'I hope you're right,' said Holly. She squared her shoulders and strode bravely towards the buggy.

The beach looked as if the party had already started.

There were real flambeaux on long poles stuck in the sand. Their flames beat sideways in the occasional gusts from the sea, a trail of smoke following the flaring light. Someone had put up a canopy. Someone else had brought a saxophone and was playing late-night blues.

And people were everywhere! Men in uniforms, men in suits, some of them even wearing ties. Men in shorts and jeans and even those loose three-quarter trousers that made them look like eighteenth-century sailors. Women in everything from cocktail glitter to business suits. Plenty of wild batik prints on men and women alike. Skins every shade from so black it was purple to treacle-gold.

Holly recorded it all as if she were going to paint it. She stared and stared until her eyes ached. It nearly took her mind off the repeating loop in her head...

I can't believe I'm doing this. I'll regret it...

Jack, of course, was already there, a tall, commanding figure in the flaring light. He was surrounded but she still saw him at once, the moment that Proteus helped her out of the car. There was a press of people but Jack was still the first—the only—person she registered.

He stood out like the king in some pagan ritual. Perhaps it was his stillness. Perhaps it was the way he turned and fixed her with his eyes like a spear. In all the shifting crowd, the wind-blown light, the waving palms, he seemed to be the only steady thing at rest on the beach. In the shadows he looked like a rock. A rock that was summoning her.

A thought flashed into her mind. *I could break myself against a rock like that.* Holly swallowed and took a couple of careful steps onto the soft sand. It felt as if the whole world was shifting under her feet.

Every single person on the beach seemed to be Jack's lifelong friend. They crowded round him, cheering him on, pleased as punch to be at his celebration.

Holly looked at the carnival crowd and realised she had never felt so lonely in her life. And she was a connoisseur of loneliness.

'Ready?' said Paula Vincent, brushing the creases out of Holly's dress.

She had been wearing the crocheted shawl against the cold but it clearly offended Paula's sense of fitness that Holly should go to the altar in it. Now Paula twitched it away. Holly felt the chill touch her naked shoulders; it was replaced by the strangeness of her wind-wafted hair, then his eyes.

Oh, God, those slanting dark eyes: so intent; so *unreadable*. For a moment, she wanted to pull the shawl back round her shoulders, as if it would hide her from him. She felt her mouth dry and her heart start to patter, light and quick and breathless.

Jack did not take his eyes off her. But he said something to a tall black man beside him. The man detached himself and took up a book. His dark clothes resolved themselves into a minister's suit and white collar.

Holly thought, *It's happening. It's really happening*. Her heartbeat was like a soft skittering roll on the bongo drums. She was the only one who could hear it. But it reverberated through her until she could not hear anything else.

As if she were in a dream. A long way away—all the way outside her head—the saxophone modified into something sweet and serious. The cheerful crowd fell silent. Her flat sandals were soundless on the damp sand. The crowd gathered, closing in behind her.

The breeze feathered her hair across her mouth. She pushed it back but it was no good. She could feel Jack watching the wafting tendrils of hair. The fragile finery of her wedding dress stirred ceaselessly. He watched that too. She thought, though she did not know why, *He wants to touch me.*

She felt cold and afraid and alone. At the same time she felt as if she were setting out on the biggest adventure of her life. And excited.

She reached Jack. How tall he was! How tall and broad and warm-blooded in the darkness! She had never felt so physically vulnerable to a man before. He did not touch her, not so much as take her hand. Yet she felt his eyes on her, as sensuous as the most deliberate caress.

He wants to touch me, she thought again.

She did not know how she knew it. She just did. With absolute certainty. She began to tremble.

But when he spoke, his tone was matter-of-fact. 'Francis, you've met Holly, I believe.'

'I have.' The minister sent a kind but faintly puzzled smile in her direction. 'Are you ready to make your vows now?'

And that was it. So simple, she slipped into it and hardly noticed. When Jack slid the ring onto her cold finger, she gave a start.

This is it.

She heard herself, Holly Anne, promise her life away to John Charles, whom she had not known a week ago. He kissed her cold cheek.

The mischievous breeze whipped her hair across his face. He turned his head to avoid it and his open mouth brushed hers.

For a moment Holly breathed his breath. The pattering drum roll stopped dead.

Something quickened inside her. Something old and yet utterly, utterly new. It was fierce and not cold at all.

Jack drew back. Was there a question in the slanting eyes? Or was that a trick of the uncertain light?

The saxophone's tune now was one of naked triumph. People were patting Jack on the back, shaking his hand, full of frank teasing. He put an arm round Holly, as if to include her in the congratulations. But it was obvious nobody really knew what to say to her. There was a distinct air of relief in the way the crowd started to dance as a steel band struck up.

Jack looked down at her, his expression unreadable.

'Are you tired?'

'Yes.' It was the truth. But would he take that as a sign that she wanted to go back to that lux-

urious cabin and be alone with him? Holly panicked. 'No. I mean—a bit, but I can... You don't
have to...'

He did not comment on that. 'Do you want to
dance at your own wedding?'

'Dance?'

She saw that he was smiling faintly. 'That's
why they brought the band, I'm afraid.'

'Oh. I thought Proteus was exaggerating.'

'Proteus never exaggerates,' he said, amused.

He put his arm round her and drew her loosely
to him. It was quite impersonal. Under the light
cotton jacket his arm felt like fire against her
floating flimsy dress, though.

Holly swallowed hard.

'This isn't quite the wedding you might have
hoped for.' His tone was dry. 'Do you mind?'

'I didn't really think much about the form of
the wedding,' Holly said honestly.

There was a pause. He moved with easy
rhythm to the music. So why did it feel as if he
had suddenly frozen in his tracks?

Then, 'No, I suppose it wasn't very important,'
he agreed. He suddenly sounded immensely
weary. Of course he must have been travelling for
twenty-odd hours. He was entitled to be weary.
So why did she feel as if a light had been turned
off?

'You seem to have a lot of friends here,' she ventured after a moment.

'Yes. More than I realised. Maybe this island was a mistake,' he said almost to himself.

Holly shook her head. 'I think it's great that you have so many people who want you to be happy. Even though this isn't a real— I mean, we may be a bit unusual…'

'You mean, even though this isn't a real marriage,' said Jack, suddenly harsh.

'Well, yes.' Holly was taken aback. 'But they don't know that. They still wish you well. I think that's terrific. I think you ought to appreciate that. And remember it always.'

His voice was cynical. 'On the cold dark nights when I'm alone?'

Holly winced. 'Don't.'

He pulled her closer. It was not affection, she realised. Nor any desire to deceive his partying friends. It was simple anger.

'You know, I never expected to spend my wedding night planning for the lonely times to come.' She had never heard that note of savagery from super-controlled Jack Armour before.

To the revellers it must have looked as if he were murmuring full-scale seduction into her ear. Only she, too close and a fellow conspirator, knew different. Her trembling increased.

She pulled back in his arms and stared up at him.

'But you knew,' she stammered. 'You agreed… It was your idea…'

For a moment his restraining arm felt like steel. Then, as suddenly as the fierce anger had struck, it seemed to dissolve. His arm relaxed. He let her go.

'Of course.' Once again he was smoothly master of himself and the situation again.

What was it Mrs Vincent had said? Jack Armour always kept his promises? For the first time it occurred to Holly: which one was he going to keep this time? His undertaking to give her the wedding certificate that would set her free? Or the promise he had just made in front of forty-odd witnesses to hold and cherish her for the rest of their lives?

'Don't look like that.' He sounded amused.

'Like what?'

'Like a gazelle that doesn't know if the tiger has eaten yet.'

'Very funny,' muttered Holly sourly.

'I take my humour where I find it.'

She looked around at the crowd. Everyone was dancing now and there was a definite smell of barbecue in the air.

'And you find it here?' She was unexpectedly hurt.

'I'm trying. Believe me, I'm trying.'

She did not ask him to explain. She did not want to know. She wanted to keep her head down and get out of the unwelcome party as soon as she decently could.

She would have managed it, too. If it hadn't been for Paula Vincent pressing a rum punch into her hand. Holly had forgotten to eat all day and it went straight to her head. Even so she could have got away, pleading tiredness. Jack would have let her go, she was sure. But people had cameras and they wanted to take pictures to remember.

'Kiss the bride,' someone called out.

Jack caught her round the waist again. As she whirled towards him, astonished and off balance, she saw his expression in a sudden flare of one of the flambeaux. It was not unreadable at all. It was devilishly challenging.

And then his mouth closed on hers.

Fire. It was like fire. Suffocating, terrifying, unstoppable. No concessions and no disguise. They were equals, adults, and their adult bodies wanted each other. Her limbs stopped taking orders from her brain.

Oh, Lord, was Holly's last coherent thought. *I should have known this would happen. How did I ever get into this? Here I go...*

CHAPTER FIVE

HE LIFTED his head.

'I wondered,' he murmured.

Holly had no doubt at all what he had wondered about. Whether she would kiss him back, obviously.

Well, now he had his answer: and so had she. With enthusiasm. With heart-stopping, terrifying abandon. With—her heart turned over—was it?—love?

How could I have let this happen?

He rubbed his thumb across her cheekbone. It was half a caress, half exploration by a new claimant. His hand felt huge. And dangerous somehow. Like a fire she had got too close to without realising.

'Nothing to say?'

Holly folded her lips together and tried to hide her miserable inexperience.

'I didn't expect—' she began, at last.

'Did you think dinosaurs don't kiss?' he asked drily.

It must have rankled, when she'd called him a dinosaur in Paris. That was the second time he had referred to it. Had she been using the image to protect herself from him? Holly she did not know. Now she met his eyes bravely.

'Not like that.'

His eyes flickered.

'So think about it.'

He gave her an enigmatic smile. And let her go.

The party took off after that. Dazed, Holly found herself congratulated, plied with colourful drinks and embraced by people who did not stop dancing to do it. All to a cheerful beat. She saw that even people who were theoretically chatting on the edge of the crowd were keeping time with their feet or their shoulders.

Jack danced all the time. But—not with her.

It was unnerving, Holly thought. He was like someone she had never met before suddenly: a bit of a wild man, free and laughing, but with a dangerous edge to his laughter. The men, she saw, admired him. To the women he was quite simply a magnet, effortless and compulsive. Even Paula Vincent, who surely believed it when she said she loved him only like a brother, put a wilder swing into her hips when she gyrated round Jack Armour.

As for Holly—all she knew was that she was out of her depth. Here he had a physical presence, a sheer sensual impact, that nothing had prepared her for. She had not the slightest idea how to deal with it.

After that mind-blowing kiss, he had simply let her go. She'd swayed. He'd steadied her, smiled down at her enigmatically and then whirled Paula Vincent away into the dance without a word. And had moved on from woman to laughing woman.

Just as well, Holly told herself. If Jack put his hands on her again she thought she just might dissolve into a puddle of warm lust at his feet. She ignored her leaping pulses and did her best to enjoy the party. Which was not easy, given that she felt that she might wake up at any moment.

Somehow she had got to the edge of the dancing crowd. Alone for a moment, she contemplated the darkness. Ahead of her the sea heaved and purred like a sleepy animal. The stars flickered, there and then not there, in the black waves. And then behind her, on the palm-fringed beach, was a challenge she did not think she was ready for.

'Time to go?' said a voice in her ear.

Holly froze. She knew that voice. The challenge was no longer behind her, dancing with other people. He was here. And ready or not, she was going to have to make a decision *fast*.

Trying to buy time, not taking her eyes off the lazy sea she said, 'Don't leave the party on my account.'

Jack gave a soft laugh. 'Now there's a thing to say to a husband on his wedding night.'

Holly's voice rose several notches. 'Please. You don't have to be polite.'

'What if I want to be—polite?'

He sounded amused. Also horribly sexy. Inexperienced as she was, Holly still recognised that. She shivered.

'See. You're cold. It *is* time to go.'

They would have to be alone together tonight. She had known they would. She had just not allowed herself to think about it. Now Holly searched about for a reason to defer the inevitable confrontation.

'But won't everyone mind?'

'Hardly.'

'But—'

'It is generally expected that the bride and groom will leave together,' he said mock solemn.

Holly jumped. That word *again*. 'I wish everyone would stop calling me a bride!' she said between her teeth.

'But you look so very bridal.'

She looked at him at last, shocked. They were out of the light of the torches here, but in the

moonlight she saw the flash of teeth in his lop-
sided smile. That smile made her feel hot all over,
then cool as a rock pool. What did he *want*?

Embarrassed, Holly muttered, 'Mrs Vincent
said I had to have a wedding dress. I'm afraid
you paid for it.'

'Money well spent,' he said lazily. He flicked
the end of one of the tresses that mantled her bare
arm. 'I didn't know you had so much hair.'

His fingers did not even touch her skin. But
she felt engulfed by electricity, as if a blue flash
had sizzled round her, cutting her out from the
night air and delivering her into another dimen-
sion where there was only Jack and Holly.

And a minefield between them.

Holly sought wretchedly for something to say
that would release the tension. There was nothing.

And the music was suddenly louder.

'Time we were not here,' Jack said lightly.

'But the party—'

'The party will probably go on till morning.'

'But I thought you hadn't seen your friends for
so long. And they put this party together for you
so quickly. They will be shocked if you leave so
soon.'

Jack was suddenly impatient. 'Believe me, the
only thing that would shock them was if you and
I were still here at sunrise.'

'Oh.'

In the darkness she was blushing furiously. Why did Jack always end up making her feel ridiculous? She was strong, independent and she could look after herself, as she had proved round half Europe. So why this clumsiness with him and only him?

I wish I knew more: more about flirting; more about when men are teasing and when they are serious; more about life.

He said gently, as if he were reading her thoughts, 'I won't push you into anything you don't want. I promise.'

Holly believed him. Which was somehow the most terrifying thing of all.

She went with him.

She had expected him to take her back through the party, to extract Proteus or one of the other drivers there and summon a taxi to take them back to the hotel. She cringed at the thought of walking through the crowd, though she was too proud to admit it. But once again Jack seemed to read her mind.

He took her away from the party, down the beach to a small group of trees. There was a beach-buggy parked under them.

'I don't know whether they were planning any practical jokes,' Jack said wryly. 'I just thought: best take no chances.'

For the first time, it seemed for days, Holly laughed naturally.

'Good thinking, Batman.'

He handed her up into the compact little vehicle. 'No, just reasonable contingency planning.' He swung in beside her and switched on the engine. 'I like to be prepared.'

'So I see.'

'And I don't like surprises.'

'I'll remember that,' she said lightly.

He switched on the headlights, raking the sand and the trees like an enemy's spotlight.

'Let's go.'

He seemed to know the roads incredibly well. Almost at once he turned off the metalled surface onto a path of impacted earth. It rolled like the sea in the headlights. The buggy bumped and lurched but Jack's hands were like iron, keeping the kicking wheel under control. Holly looked at the muscles in his forearms and the long, strong fingers and felt again how alien he seemed, out here in the Caribbean night.

They came into the hotel complex by a path she did not know.

'It's the far cabin,' she said. Her voice sounded unnaturally loud to her.

'I know.'

She blinked. 'How?'

'I asked Paula.'

'Oh.' She digested that and could make nothing of it. 'Why?'

Jack laughed. 'I thought with all the rum punch you were downing, you might not be in any condition to navigate us home.'

Home. It sounded odd. Holly had not had a home, a real home, for so long. And Jack did not have one at all; did not even seem to feel the lack of one. Yet suddenly here he was calling a little plantation cabin where they would spend just one night 'home'. It was crazy. Yet somehow it felt right.

Impulsively she turned to him.

'Jack?'

'Yes?'

'Thank you.'

He swung the buggy into the lea of the cottage and cut the engine.

'No need to thank me. I please myself.'

She shook her head. 'No, you don't. You never wanted to marry me. I knew it, even when you were saying it was the only solution. You didn't say it but I knew that you thought I should have faced them. I shouldn't have said yes...'

Jack looked down at her. 'Second thoughts? It's a bit late for that.'

Holly said vehemently, 'No second thoughts.'

His eyes gleamed in the moonlight. 'Then let's go inside.'

He leaped lightly down from the buggy and came round to help her. It was no more than a courtesy. He just touched her hand as she stepped out of the vehicle. But Holly could have sworn that his fingers burned her palm.

The bongo drums started under her ribcage again. She put a hand to her head.

'What is it?' said Jack swiftly.

He slipped an arm round her waist to steady her. That was worse. His strength seemed to flow through her, imprinting her.

Why is my body reacting like this? thought Holly, frantic.

But she could not say that. Not aloud. Not to Jack. She searched for something he would believe and her eyes fell on the tall bush of trumpet flowers that tumbled over the end of the verandah.

Seizing the excuse gratefully, she said, 'The scent of those flowers. It made my head swim for a moment.'

His look was shrewd. 'Do you want me to carry you?'

'*No!*'

He laughed. It was an amazingly sensual sound.

'Well, lean on me, then, my bride.'

And Holly had no choice but to do just that. It made her legs tremble as if she was going to pass out. *What is happening to me?* she thought.

He produced a key to the cabin.

'How did you get that? I left mine at the desk.'

'Forward planning again. I told Paula to bring it with her. I thought you would want to come straight back here, rather than go collecting keys at the desk.' He unlocked the door and swept her inside, pausing to look down on her only when he had closed the door. 'Was I wrong?'

Outside the cicadas were thrumming like the percussion section of a full orchestra. So why did it sound like thunder when she swallowed?

'N-no.'

He snapped the light switch. It turned on three table lamps, their soft light pooling around the huge four-poster bed.

He looked down at her.

'I never noticed before.' He sounded taken aback. 'Your eyes are like marmalade.'

'Lovely,' said Holly with irony. But she shivered with pleasure to have him look at her like that.

He touched the corner of one eye very gently. 'It is. All green and gold.'

Still in the comparative shadows of the door, Holly could not read his expression, though she searched his face like an explorer in new terrain.

Jack seemed to make up his mind. He turned, masking her with his body. Putting his hands either side of her head, he leaned towards her.

'And am I wrong about this too?' he murmured.

Holly found herself arching towards him. It was a long, long kiss.

Her feelings bewildered her. She had not known such sensations were possible, Her mouth felt fuller, softer, infinitely more responsive than she had ever imagined. When Jack raised his head and murmured, 'Mmm, sweet,' she knew exactly what he meant.

He brushed her hair back from her naked shoulders. Holly shivered. Her skin seemed suddenly to have become super-sensitive. She held her breath as he bent his head. When—with excruciating slowness—he touched the tip of his tongue to the heated skin, she gave a low moan of pure need.

He smiled down at her, his eyes so tender she barely recognised him. And then he put her away from him with a rueful smile. He stepped back...

No, screamed her heart.

She swayed towards him. Her body felt light and vulnerable. He caught her by the shoulders, holding her at arm's length.

'Not a good idea,' he said unevenly. 'I shouldn't have kissed you.'

Holly closed her eyes. She had a vision of herself as a leaf, tossed and rushed and spun about, half drowned in the ferocity of a waterfall. By contrast, Jack felt like a rock. And she needed to haul herself up on that rock or she would die.

She inserted herself under his guard and clung like a magnet.

'Holly!' He sounded strangled.

Ignoring his resistance, she reached up. He avoided her blindly seeking lips.

'Stop a moment. *Think!'* His chest was lifting and falling as if it hurt. 'I promised you a marriage of convenience.'

Holly was breathing as if she had just run up the hill from the Place des Abbesses. She opened her eyes and shook her head, trying to clear it. 'What?'

'You didn't sign up for this. And nor, God help me, did I.'

Her blood drummed. He was distracted, utterly unlike cool, controlled Jack Armour. Had she done that to him?

Holly's lips parted. He looked shaken to the core.

'Stop looking at me like that!' he said in a voice she hardly recognised.

She said his name, voiceless. It was a plea. She did not quite know what she was begging for.

Jack did, though. As if he could not help himself, he hauled her tight against him and suddenly he was kissing her fiercely.

Holly made a small sound, half-fear, half-exhilaration. A thought flashed: *I wish I knew what to do next.*

He seemed to know the fastenings of the new dress better than she did. The white stuff fell to the floor with a soft shushing sound, revealing its secret.

He made a sound as if he had walked into a wall.

When Paula had taken her shopping, neither of them had thought about underwear. When she'd been getting ready, Holly had found that the wide drawstring neck of the wedding dress had shown the strap of every one of the three bras she possessed. So there had been only one solution. Now

he held her away from him and Holly's breath
stopped at the look in his eyes.

'This,' he said raggedly, 'is not fair. I'm trying
to be chivalrous.'

As if of their own volition, his fingers began to
undo his shirt. He was clumsy in his haste. Jack,
who was never clumsy.

He never took his eyes off her, never for one
second. And suddenly Holly felt beautiful. Shy
and proud and beautiful all at the same time.

She watched him rip his clothes away and
thought: *It's all right. I do know what to do next,
after all.*

Her panties were thin with much washing. She
slipped out of them and left them there on the
floor as she walked into his arms.

But even then he held back for one last, agon-
ising second.

'Holly,' he said, on a shaken note.

She thought she felt his mouth on her hair.

'Are you sure?' It was so quiet she hardly
heard him. 'Oh, God, I shouldn't do this. You
don't know what you're doing.'

She pressed closer, looking up to meet his eyes.
Her mouth trembled. Then, very deliberately, she
ran her open palms down the taut back. She felt
the muscles clench under her caress and smiled.

'Don't I?'

He went completely still. For a terrible moment Holly thought he was going to resist after all. She shook back her head so that her hair fell and brushed the arms so tight around her.

If he doesn't make love to me now, I'll die. She was not sure that she had not said it aloud.

He let out a long, uneven breath. And then he was lifting her, carrying her, taking her to that bed in its pool of light...

She learned that Jack Armour was a leisurely lover. She learned that he took pleasure seriously. He explored her body with meticulous sensuality, refusing to be deflected by shyness, inexperience, or even her longing to please him in turn.

'Do you like that?' the low voice would demand. And until she answered he would leave her in the exquisite torture of suspense.

'Yes,' she gasped in the end.

'And that? That?'

'Yes. Oh, yes.'

The total intimacy of it was terrifying. And yet somehow straight out of her dreams. Holly felt she had been waiting for this place, this time, all her life.

Her own body turned into a wild creature she did not recognise. It was Jack whom she knew. Jack who steadied and held her, even while his touch drove her crazy. Jack whom she could trust.

Very gently, he shifted her hips. She held her breath, not quite believing it. And then she felt him inside her. Holly screwed her eyes tight shut, turning her head on the pillow, waiting...

'Holly.'

How could he sound so calm?

He took her head between both hands, stilling her frenzy.

'Holly, look at me.'

She opened her eyes reluctantly. He was looking at her with heart-stopping tenderness. She hardly recognised enigmatic Jack Armour.

'Don't look so worried.' He brushed her hair back from her face carefully. 'There is no easy way to do this. But I promise—*I promise*—I won't leave you unsatisfied.'

She was bewildered. 'Wh-what?'

There was a sudden sharp pain and she realised what he was talking about. She gasped. Her shocked pulses went into overdrive.

It was utterly strange, utterly new. At the same time it was so familiar that, deep under the clamour of her pulses, her blood knew she had come home. Holly soared, crying out in amazement.

'*Yes,*' said Jack.

And stopped being gentle.

*   *   *

Holly came awake with a jump. She had been dreaming and cobwebs of the nightmare still clung to her. Brendan had caught up with her, and although she had tried to run she had been staked to the spot somehow. The police had been raking her with a spotlight…

Her eyes focused. Why was the light on? Why were there so many lights? Come to that, where was she?

She tried to move and found she was pinned down, in truth. Panic flared momentarily. But then she turned her head and remembered.

Jack had collapsed into a deep, deep sleep. One arm was flung over her possessively. His bare shoulders were smooth and golden.

Holly ran a wondering hand over the compact flesh. Closing her eyes, she inhaled dreamily.

My husband. Who would have thought it?

He stirred, muttering, but did not wake. Well, of course not. He had been travelling for the best part of twenty-four hours even before the wedding. Holly felt a great surge of tenderness. Carefully, so as not to wake him, she reached out and snapped off the lights. Then she eased the sheet from under their bodies and pulled it over them.

At last, greatly daring, she lifted his head and cradled it to her breast. He murmured something—maybe her name?—and perhaps he kissed her breast. Holly smiled and stroked his hair a little, warm in the friendly dark. Then she, too, fell asleep. This time there were no nightmares.

In the morning she awoke slowly. This time she knew exactly where she was. The doors to the cabin verandah were open and the sun streamed in, outlining the dark shadow of the man standing out there, silently watching the distant sea.

Holly struggled up on one elbow, shading her eyes.

'Jack?'

He came into the little room. He was fully dressed in chinos and a green bush shirt. He brought the smell of the sea with him and the cool air of the morning.

'Oh, you're awake, are you?' His face was in shadow but his voice sounded strained.

Something about it made her say, 'Is anything wrong?'

'No. But we haven't got a lot of time if you're going to have breakfast and still make the Miami flight.'

She said slowly, 'If *I'm* going to have breakfast?'

'I've eaten,' he said curtly. 'I woke at dawn. I always do. I went across to the hotel and had something and then got on with my work.'

Why should that be hurtful? Yet it was.

Holly said, 'I'm sorry...' before she realised she did not know what she was apologising for.

Jack got even brisker, if possible. 'No reason. You needed your sleep. But I think you should be moving soon.'

Not a kiss, not a touch, and yards of polished parquet flooring between them. All that care for her last night. All that tenderness... And now it seemed as if he would hardly look at her. What had happened?

She shook her head, bewildered. 'Why?'

'I told you. The plane.'

Did he misunderstand her deliberately? Of course, she had never had a lover before. Maybe this was what every man was like the morning after. Maybe he was embarrassed by the passion he had shown her last night. Maybe—and this was a lot worse to face—he was embarrassed by the passion *she* had shown.

Holly snatched the cotton sheet up to her throat.

'I'll get up now,' she said in a strangled voice.

He seemed to hesitate. Or was that her imagination? It did not matter because almost at once
he nodded.

'I'll see you on the breakfast terrace.'

She scrambled out of bed, winding the sheet
round her so tight she hobbled herself. It was
crazy. He had looked at every inch of her last
night. But now she was wrapping herself up like
a mummy in case he caught a glimpse of breast
or thigh and was offended.

Jack turned away abruptly.

Holly felt as if she had been winded. So she
did offend him. She writhed mentally. If only she
had more experience. If only she had known what
he expected last night...

One hand on the door jamb, Jack looked over
his shoulder.

Holly did not know it but she was standing in
a beam of sunlight which struck rainbow lights
from her tumbled hair. The muscle in Jack's jaw
locked.

'Hol—'

Her drooping head lifted. 'Yes?'

He said with constraint, 'Do you think you
could pack before you come over for breakfast?'

She stared at him as if she did not recognise
him. 'Wh-what? Why?'

'So I can send over for the bags while you eat. Then we can go straight to the airport.'

'Airport? You're getting rid of me so soon?'

She thought his face twisted. But he looked away at once and she realised she must be wrong.

'Of course not.' He was brisk again. 'Damn it, I knew we should have talked last night.

There was a moment's disbelieving silence.

Then—'Talked?' She could not help herself. All her hurt, all her bewilderment were in her voice.

'It would have been more sensible than what we did do,' said Jack, suddenly savage.

Holly's whole body flinched from the cruelty of it. But he was looking out across the hibiscus bushes and did not see.

He went on, 'But we can't do anything about that now. We have to think of what's best for you. I gather you haven't made any plans?'

Holly shook her head. She was having difficulty in adjusting to this new Jack. Or rather not a new Jack. This was the old Jack, cool as an arctic breeze and with roughly the same effect.

'Was I supposed to make plans?' she said, distracted. 'I didn't realise... I'm sorry.'

'No sweat. If you'd planned something, then I wouldn't want you to change it.'

Wouldn't you? Why wouldn't you? She did not quite have the courage to say it aloud.

After all, maybe making love as they had last night was no big deal for him. Maybe he had made love to hundreds of women like that.

She swallowed. 'What do you suggest?'

'I've got to go back to Ignaz. You could come along. We could use an extra pair of hands. Do you speak Spanish?'

'Yes.'

'Then you'll be useful.'

Oh, yes, that was the old Jack all right, logical and realistic. Holly could have wept. Her chin came up.

'It sounds a good practical plan,' she said quietly. 'Give me ten minutes.'

The hotel was famous for its breakfasts: fresh mango and pineapple and guava, served with home made rolls and wonderful fragrant coffee. Holly looked at the food as if it would choke her and barely touched the coffee.

'Hangover?' said Jack, not without sympathy. He poured water for her from a jug steaming with ice. 'The local rum punch is lethal. I should have warned you.'

She looked up quickly. 'Is that what's wrong?'

She looked very young in her cotton T-shirt, her hair in its curly fronded plait again. Jack looked away painfully.

'Wrong?'

She looked at him very directly. Her eyes were very dark this morning, no trace of last night's golden green.

'I've done something wrong,' she said bravely. 'Just *tell* me. What is it?'

He did not pretend to misunderstand her this time. 'Not you, Holly. Me.'

'What? I don't understand.'

'I know you don't. That's what makes it so unforgivable.'

She did not understand him.

'Do you regret last night, then?'

A muscle leaped in Jack's jaw. 'It is not a question of regret,' he said curtly. 'I broke the agreement.'

And Paula Vincent had said he always kept his word. Holly began to see what might be the matter.

'I wanted you to break it,' she reminded him softly.

The slanting eyes were black. It almost looked as if he was in pain.

'You were not thinking straight. And I knew it. I just chose to ignore it.'

'Does thinking matter? About *that*?'

'When you're older,' said Jack deliberately, 'you'll find that thinking is essential. Particularly about *that*.'

Holly winced. But she was brave enough. She had had to be and now, if ever, was the time to face up to what she had done.

'And if I told you I don't regret it?'

For a moment his eyes seemed to soften. Then he shook his head.

'It makes no difference. Sex wasn't part of the deal.'

'But—'

He interrupted. 'For either of us.'

'Ah.' She digested that in silence for a moment. 'You're saying you didn't want me.'

'Of course I'm not saying that,' he said impatiently.

'We-ell...'

'I wanted you so badly I broke all my own rules,' he said harshly. 'OK?'

That made her feel a bit better.

'That's what I thought last night,' she said.

She met his eyes very directly. Jack's face did not move but she thought he whitened under that wonderful golden skin.

'So how do I make you feel this morning?'

There was a shuddering pause.

Then he said, 'Old.'

Holly was shocked. It showed.

With a muttered oath he got up and walked over to the balustrade. She could see the tension in the back of his neck.

She almost said, Would it have been all right if I hadn't been a virgin? Almost.

Not looking at her, he said, 'It shouldn't have happened. We were both tired. And you'd had too much of their devil's brew. I knew that. There's no excuse for me.'

And then, like a hammer-blow, 'It won't happen again.'

CHAPTER SIX

THE extraordinary thing about Jack Armour, thought Holly, was how totally he could disguise his feelings when he wanted to. In the last twelve hours she had seen him break through his cool façade into passion that took her breath away. She had seen him furious with regret, too.

But when they arrived at the little airport, to a hero's send-off, you would have thought that he was a happy bridegroom looking forward to a life of conjugal bliss.

Holly was not that good a liar. Jack's words kept going round and round in her head, drowning out the chat and the laughter: *It won't happen again. It won't happen again.*

Jack seemed to have put the whole conversation out of his mind. Holly could not. She could not help it. She held herself stiff under his encircling arm and answered the well-meaning questions in monosyllables.

Shy, the islanders said kindly, and gave her a large straw hat to hide her blushes. But Jack knew she was not shy. He was impatient.

'Come on,' he said in her ear as he held her in front of him to wave at the crowd of well-wishers. 'They've done their best for us. You can give them a smile.'

Holly tried. She really tried. But that cruel mockery of an embrace felt like chains on her heart. Her wave was as mechanical as clockwork.

Jack held her away from him, smiling. All his mates from the hurricane loved it. They did not see, as Holly did, that the smile did not reach his eyes.

'You can do better than that,' he told her. 'Blow them a kiss.'

She managed not to glare at him. She was weeping inside but she was not going to let him see that either.

'I'm all out of kisses,' she told him with a sweet, false smile.

His eyes narrowed. 'Oh, no, you're not.'

He kissed her. Hard.

To the delighted watchers, it must have looked like the extreme of passion. To Holly, clamped to a body as unyielding as steel, it carried an altogether different message.

I may have wanted you last night, it said. *But don't think that means anything. Never forget: it won't happen again.*

She felt physically broken. It was as if Jack had extracted some essential part of her last night without realising it and in the muddle of the morning it had smashed beyond repair.

I suppose this is what they mean by a broken heart, thought Holly.

The mouth on hers felt angry. Or maybe it didn't. Maybe that was her inexperience misleading her. Again.

She could not bear any more. She removed herself from his embrace. It seemed to her—but maybe that was an illusion too—that his arms tightened possessively for a moment before he let her go. But then he was turning her back to the crowd, making her wave and smile.

A small girl tottered through the barrier bearing a bright hibiscus flower. She looked up at Holly doubtfully, then cast a scared glance over her shoulder at her encouraging mother. Holly could hardly see through her tears but the child's uncertainty touched her. She went down on one knee and took the flower.

'Thank you.'

Holly felt helpless. She knew nothing about children. Her mother had never had the time for other people's babies and Donna was childless. She knew the child was alarmed by her swimming eyes but she did not know what to say to reassure her.

It was not a problem for Jack, though. He scooped the little one up easily and set her on his shoulder. 'What's your name, honey?'

The child beamed, relieved. 'Felicia.'

'Pretty name for a pretty lady,' said Jack easily.

He took her back to the barrier and handed her over to the proud mother. 'You've got a star there, ma'am.'

Holly got to her feet unnoticed. By the time he came back she had blinked the tears away.

He still said, as they were going through passport control and security, 'You all right?'

'I'm fine,' said Holly.

She went on saying it all day. From Sugar Island to Barbados. From Barbados to Miami, to San Antonio. Eventually she was saying it in a lurching Jeep going up a mud-encrusted mountainside.

'Say something else, for God's sake,' said Jack, losing his cool self-control at last. 'I know you're not fine. You've made it plain enough. Why don't you just admit it?'

But Holly was not admitting anything.

'I need some time to adjust, that's all.'

She aimed a pleasant smile at his right ear. As long as she did not meet those dark searching eyes, she told herself, she would be all right. Eventually.

She was aware of their driver looking at them in the mirror.

In fact, Holly's arrival had clearly thrown their driver badly. Outside the airport, Jack had refused to slip into the driving seat as the man obviously expected him to. Instead he had firmly stepped into the back seat beside his new wife. Ever since Holly had been trying to avoid his eyes, to say nothing of his too casual, too indifferent touch. And he knew it.

Now he muttered something impatient.

She looked down at the hibiscus blossom she had carried all through the various customs and immigration checks. Its golden glory was gone. Now it looked like a piece of brown rag.

'Sad,' she said, changing the subject deliberately. 'Doesn't travel well, obviously. I should have put it in water.'

He sent her a shrewd look. 'Hibiscus blossoms die at night. Water would have made no difference.'

'Oh?' She put the withered blossom carefully into her waist pouch. 'Like me,' she said trying to lighten the atmosphere. 'We can do glamour but only until the clock strikes.'

'You can do glamour whenever you want to,' he said with unexpected softness.

He pulled her plait forward over her shoulder. At once Holly stiffened in pure instinct.

'Relax,' he said, frowning.

But he took his hand away.

When they stopped, he swung quickly out of the Jeep and held out a hand to her before the driver could get out of his seat. Holly pretended she did not see the offered hand. She climbed out of the Jeep unaided and found her legs buckling under her.

'Hang on,' said Jack.

He caught her competently and restored her to her feet. Holly's eyes flew to his face. She was shocked at the way her heart bounded in her breast at even this most disinterested of embraces.

'Altitude shock,' he told her with a faint smile. 'Don't worry. You'll get used to it.'

'W-will I?'

'We all do. The only question is how long it takes.'

Which gave her the perfect opening to ask what she had been thinking about all the time on their silent journey.

'Am I staying here long enough to get used to it?'

Jack's smile was enigmatic. 'Up for discussion.'

Which of course was no help at all. Holly could have screamed. Only then he let her go and she was too busy standing upright on legs that felt as if they were made of candy-floss to do anything as energetic as screaming.

Jack made sure that she was not actually going to slip sideways into the mud before turning back to the Jeep. He swung the bags out of the back and looped the strap of her roll bag over his shoulder as if he had been doing it all his life. As if the bag belonged to him. As if, thought Holly, leaning against the muddy car in a breathless daze, *she* belonged to him.

It gave her the strangest feeling. As if he had some sort of rights in her and she did belong to him, somehow.

Shocked, she took herself to task. *It's too long since I belonged to anybody,* Holly thought, alarmed. *That's all it is. Too many years of loneliness and too much high-octane illusion yesterday. I will get over this.*

But she avoided his touch when he tried to steady her as they made their way up a path of duck boarding, even when she lurched and nearly stumbled.

'Stupid,' she said instead, brightly. 'Where is this?'

Jack's hand fell to his side.

'Ignaz's answer to the Ritz,' he said drily. 'You'll be sharing my tent, of course.'

'Of course,' said Holly coolly, though her heart's instant reaction nearly made her stumble again. She looked round the sea of tents. 'In these circumstances I wouldn't dream of anything else.'

'Good girl,' said Jack, unexpectedly.

He took her into the command post and introduced her rapidly. Holly got about four names before her jet-lagged brain gave out but she thought she would recognise most of the faces again.

'And Ramon, of course, you know,' Jack ended.

Ramon put aside the map he was studying and shook hands.

'Good to see you.' He seemed genuinely welcoming. His next words explained why. 'We can really use another interpreter.'

Holly was worried. 'I hope Jack hasn't misled you. I'm OK in colloquial Spanish but I haven't got any language qualifications or anything.'

Ramon grinned. 'As long as you can count and kick ass that will do.'

'Count?'

'Ten trucks. Five thousand shots of antibiotic. That sort of thing.'

Holly relaxed. 'I can probably manage that.'

'And it's about time you learned to kick ass,' Jack agreed blandly. He put that proprietorial arm round her again and moved her out of the tent. 'Rules: we don't go out of the camp alone. The land may still be unstable. On the street, don't eat anything uncooked unless you can peel it. Report any injuries or fever immediately. And no hair-washing.'

She stopped. 'What?'

He grinned down at her. 'We only use water for essentials. You've got too much hair. Keep it up out of the way and it won't be too bad.'

Holly pulled a face. But she did not demur. She could see how precious water must be here.

He pulled her plait. 'I promise you the best power shower in Miami when I ship you out.'

'I look forward to it,' she said with feeling.

His grin widened, almost as if he shared her anticipation. Holly stared at him suspiciously. At once he turned businesslike, leading the way off on a spur of duckboard.

'My tent is over here.'

Holly followed perforce. But, if anything, her suspicions increased. Was that a twitch at the corner of his mouth? Was he amusing himself privately at her expense?

He pushed aside a heavy canvas flap and she stepped up onto a prefabricated floor of some sort. The tent had the bare essentials—two low beds with sleeping bags on them and a stalk with a lantern on it. Old banana crates seemed to serve for everything else from storage to a writing surface.

Holly swallowed. She had travelled on a shoe-string and thought she had lived in some pretty poor places. She had never come anywhere near this.

'Basic,' she said lightly.

Jack tossed her roll bag onto a crate.

'You should have seen what it was like when we first got here.'

That sobered her. She had seen the news footage on friends' televisions.

'I can imagine.'

'And hard beds are good for your back.' He swung his own case onto his bed and was unpacking with the speed of long practice. Over his shoulder he added, 'Anyway, you're so tired you're asleep before you hit the bed.'

Holly unzipped her roll bag. 'I can imagine,' she said again. 'And whose bed will I be hitting?'

He turned round, one wicked eyebrow raised. Furious, Holly found she was blushing to her hairline. She began to flounder.

'I mean—two beds... Someone must have... You can't have had a tent to yourself. Who were you with...? *Oh, damn!*'

She threw a pair of rolled-up socks at the tent wall. They bounced back.

Jack took pity on her.

'Ramon. And before you ask, no, I didn't kick him out. He decided to move on all on his own.'

'I know you didn't kick him out,' muttered Holly, her cheeks still burning.

Had he not said to her only this morning, 'It won't happen again'? Would she ever forget it? Jack was the last person to make sure that they shared their sleeping arrangements. He was going to hate it almost as much as she was.

'We'll just have to live with it,' she said, pursuing the thought upper most in her mind.

There was the tiniest pause.

'You'll get used to it. In fact, pretty soon you'll be too tired to notice,' Jack assured her pleasantly.

It gave her the perfect alibi.

'I think I'm too tired now.' Holly gave an enormous and not entirely contrived yawn. 'It's been a long day.'

He looked at his watch. 'The daily briefing is nearly due. We all go to that. Afterwards you can eat with the rest of us or come back here and sleep, as you choose.'

The briefing, Holly found, was an informal affair and as quick as the participants could decently manage. Today there was some slippage of one of the spurs of duckboard; the doctors were asking for an isolation tent; the water purification system was having problems. The weather, however, looked set to improve. And there were more visitors coming up from the capital tomorrow.

'Holly can translate,' said Ramon, who was leading the meeting. He looked across at her. 'OK?'

'I'll do my best.'

He came over to her when the meeting dispersed.

'How do you like bean stew?'

'Fine, I suppose,' she said surprised.

'Because that's the evening meal. The Emergency Relief people gave us those little packets of reconstituted food that astronauts use. But frankly the water is too precious. So the women keep a cauldron bubbling. If there's anything in it apart from beans, I haven't come across it.'

'Sounds interesting.'

He took her arm to guide her to the communal tent.

'Did anyone think to give you a torch?'

'Not yet.'

'You'll need it. Even in daylight, sometimes, we're getting strange cloud shut-down. I'll bring you one over. Jack tell you the rules?'

Holly found herself tensing instinctively. But she answered steadily enough. 'Yes. He's been very—conscientious.'

Ramon sniffed. 'Conscientious. Great. Just what you want on your honeymoon.'

She turned to him. 'Ramon, will you tell me something?'

He looked uneasy. 'If it's about Jack, you'd better ask him.'

'I can't.'

His uneasiness increased. 'Why not?'

'I can't *pry*. It's not that sort of marriage.' She looked at him very straightly. 'You know it's not that sort of marriage.'

His eyes were the first to fall. 'All right,' he said at last, resigned. 'What do you want to know?'

Holly hesitated. 'Who was she?'

Ramon muttered again. 'You mean someone's told you about Susana. I knew they would. I told him…'

'Susana.' Holly tasted the name. 'Susana who?'

He looked round at the darkening sky. 'Not here. Let's go to my tent. At least I can give you something to burn out the taste of the beans.'

There were three beds in Ramon's tent but it was empty of people. He excavated a flat bottle from a pile of papers and offered it to her.

'No glasses.'

She unscrewed it and took the smallest possible mouthful. And coughed until her eyes watered.

'What is *that*?'

'Local cane spirit. Sort of rum. Good antiseptic in a crisis.'

'I believe it,' said Holly, blowing her nose.

Ramon grinned. 'Cures everything from manic depression to gall stones, so the locals say.'

She smiled but it was perfunctory. 'Am I going to need it?'

If he thought it odd that Jack's wife in this unemotional marriage deal should ask such a question, he did not say so. Holly suspected that for Ramon marriage was marriage and curiosity about a husband's past life came with the package. She also had a nasty feeling that he expected any woman who married Jack Armour to fall in love with him, no matter what public disclaimers they issued.

She set her teeth. 'I'm not in love with him, you understand,' she announced. 'I just don't like being the only one in the place who doesn't *know*.'

Ramon sighed. He took the bottle back and gave himself a heartening swig.

'OK. Jack had a thing going a couple of years ago with a woman in Colombia. Susana Montijo. She was a teacher, but during the earthquake he took her on as an interpreter. For a while we all thought it was serious but in the end it just—' He made an expressive gesture which dissolved the affair into thin air.

'And?'

'And what?' he said irritably.

'How long did it last? Who broke it up? What was she like?'

'Come on, Holly. You know guys don't talk about stuff like that.'

'But you knew her?'

Ramon agreed reluctantly that he'd known her.

'So what did you think? Did you like her?'

He was surprised into pulling a sour face. 'Not a lot, no. She was too much of a Mona Lisa for me.'

'What does that mean?'

He twiddled the top of the spirit bottle. 'Oh— you know. All silent suffering and making the rest of the world apologise because she had a bad start.' He looked up and Holly suddenly realised that she had touched on a slow-burning anger that he had been nursing for a long time. 'She had Jack on his knees. When they broke up he looked like death for months.'

Holly could have gasped aloud, it hurt so much. Ramon was brooding too hard on his memories to notice.

She said slowly, 'You're very fond of him, aren't you?'

Ramon looked uncomfortable. 'He's a good boss.'

She swallowed. 'One more question. Did he want to marry her?'

'Oh, yes,' said Ramon. He sounded furious. 'He wanted to marry her all right. Bought her the dream castle in England and everything. Even a ring.'

Holly stuffed her left hand into her trouser pocket as if she had burned it.

'So what happened?'

'She wouldn't make up her mind. Kept telling him to go. Then calling him back at a moment's notice. Even after the Colombian job was finished. She had no conscience. She'd pull him out of India, or Macedonia or anywhere, it didn't matter. In the end she went back to her husband.

Didn't even have the courage to tell Jack. He just walked in on them.'

Holly sat bolt upright. 'She was married? And Jack *knew*?'

'She was supposed to be divorced. But if you ask me, it was a lie from the beginning. She told him this big story about her little brothers and sisters and the old grandmother she was responsible for and he paid their bills while the husband was away working in Venezuela. That's my opinion.'

Holly was shocked. 'Jack couldn't love a woman like that!'

'Men,' said Ramon bitterly, 'can love a woman like Medusa. It's just a matter of hormones and timing.'

'But—so calculating. Surely he would see through her.'

Ramon said with great deliberation, 'Jack has a strong protective streak. He thought she needed rescuing.'

Holly froze where she sat.

'Are you telling me I'm a substitute for Susana Montijo?' she said at last.

'Of course not.' Ramon sounded shocked. And then delivered the death-cut. 'He was in love with her.'

It was dark outside when Holly left. She was grateful for the torch as she made her way back to their tent. The camp looked bigger and more threatening than it had by day.

Jack was tapping away at his laptop. He looked up when she went in.

'What happened to you? I lost you.'

'I had a drink with Ramon.'

'Oh?' His brows twitched together.

Holly sensed disapproval. 'He's the only person I know here.'

'You know me.'

But Holly was still reeling from finding out about Susana Montijo, who had had Jack on his knees for months.

'Do I?'

His frown deepened. 'That doesn't sound good. Want to talk about it?'

Holly shook her head violently.

He attacked the keyboard with a couple of vicious stabs. There was a musical tone and he switched it off, snapped it shut and put it on one side.

Holly watched, trying to block out Ramon's words. *He was in love with her. He was in love with her.* She fought for self-control.

After all, what did it matter if Jack had been in love with a woman in the past? What did it matter if he had not told her? Why should he tell her? He was not in love with Holly, after all. He might have wanted her, briefly and to his own retrospective regret. But that was all. He had made that plain only this morning.

It won't happen again.

If she was honest, that was worse even than anything that Ramon had said. That was the splinter she could not pull out of her heart.

'What's wrong?' Jack said quietly.

Holly pulled herself together. She rubbed her eyes. 'Tired, I suppose.'

'It's been a long day.' It sounded as if he was agreeing with her but the watchful eyes were not agreeing to anything. They were on patrol.

In case I try to make him break his vow of abstinence? Holly laughed aloud at the thought. There was an edge of hysteria to it that even she recognised.

Jack made an instinctive move towards her but she flung up a hand. He stopped dead.

'Sorry,' she said, turning away. 'Too much continent-hopping. I'm not used to it, like you are.'

'Oh, is that what it is?' he said drily.

'Of course. I'll be better after a decent night's sleep.'

Which, of course, opened up a whole ravine of memories of exactly what sort of sleep they had had the night before. Holly felt herself falling into the trap, even before she had finished speaking. The silence behind her was eloquent. She shut her eyes.

'*Hell*. Why don't I think before I open my mouth?' she said wretchedly.

The silence stretched.

Then he said in a level voice. 'It is a difficult situation. For both of us.'

He seemed to be waiting. What did he want her to say? Do?

It won't happen again.

Out of his sight, Holly pressed her knotted fist against her lips to stop herself crying out with the pain of it.

He said with constraint, 'You need some privacy. I have to talk to Ramon anyway. I will leave you.' He paused, then, when she did not answer, said in a low voice, 'I told you once. You don't have to do anything you don't want to. Remember that.'

Holly whirled. But the tent flap was already falling gently behind him.

He did not come back for hours.

By the time he did, Holly had stopped waiting for him. She extinguished the light and climbed into the sleeping bag. She could not sleep, though. Her thoughts kept racing. And any time they showed signs of letting up, her memory clocked in to do torture duty instead.

She had him on his knees. Holly turned over, trying to find a comfortable position.

She could not imagine Jack on his knees to anyone. Certainly not her. Last night he had tried to resist her. It was she—her whole body burned—who had forced the issue in the end. Though he had been too chivalrous to point it out this morning.

He was in love with her. The rudimentary beds were hard. She turned again.

Oh, she could imagine Jack in love, all right. He would be single-minded about it, as he was about everything else. Why, he had made love to her last night with such intensity that she could, if she hadn't known better, have mistaken it for love. When he was really in love he would put his heart and soul into it as well.

It won't happen again.

Just as well.

The sleeping bag was hopelessly tangled. Holly turned again restlessly, pushing it away with impatient fingers. And the flap parted and Jack walked in.

She could not hide the fact that she was awake. She could not hide the fact that she was looking at him. Though it was too dark for him to read her face, her whole body must have given her away. Did it give away her longing, too?

In two strides he was there. He hauled her against him. His hands were hard and his mouth was frighteningly hungry.

Holly kicked herself free of the corkscrew of bedding. Her hands on his body were as fierce as his, as shamelessly demanding. In utter silence, they fell on each other. Even when her hair caught on a button of the shirt he was throwing off, she did not make a sound. Silently, frantically, they drove each other to the mountain peak. And jumped.

In the morning Jack had gone. His sleeping bag was neatly folded on the other bed and there was a note on top of it.

Gone with the geologists. Ramon or Manolita Sanchez will tell you what to do.

Holly put the note down. No affection there. Not a word to show that last night had meant anything; that their marriage meant anything. No one would even guess that they were friends from the curt little message.

And perhaps we aren't friends. Perhaps we have gone straight from strangers to adversaries. Or, worse—perhaps when he made me his wife he turned me into a burden.

It was a chilling thought.

Holly took herself to task. There was no point in dwelling on it. She needed to get on with her life. Getting out of bed would be a start.

She negotiated her way through the bathroom arrangements, taking care to observe all the warnings about saving water. Then she went back down the hill.

Ramon was on his way out. But he steered her towards coffee and a woman with a mobile phone and a harassed expression.

'The translator,' this person greeted Holly. 'Boy, am I glad to see you. You can't manage French, I suppose?'

So started one of the longest days of Holly's life.

She interpreted for the international party of visitors. She checked supplies. She helped cook. She translated a circuit diagram and then took three local workers and a Finnish engineer through the results.

By the time night was falling, as Jack had predicted, she was so tired she could hardly keep her eyes open.

'I couldn't eat a thing,' she told Ramon when he urged her to come to dinner.

He looked at her shrewdly. 'People been asking awkward questions about you and Jack?'

Holly was betrayed into unwariness. 'Only me.'

'What?'

She recovered herself. 'Nothing. I'm talking in my sleep here.'

'Well, if you're sure…'

'I am.' She turned away and then stopped, hesitating. 'Have you seen Jack?' she said as casually as she could manage.

Ramon was too tired to notice the undercurrent. He pushed a hand through his dusty hair.

'He was going upstream with the exploration party. Doubt if they'll be back tonight.'

'Not tonight?'

Holly spun round. She was shocked and it showed.

'Depends what they find, of course. But the aerial photographs showed a lot of damage.' He frowned. 'Didn't he tell you?'

'He told me zip,' said Holly curtly. 'Is it dangerous?'

Even Ramon picked up the undercurrent this time.

'Hey, it's an experienced team. Jack can take care of himself.'

Holly glared at him in the dusk. 'Thank you for sharing that with me.'

She turned on her heel and marched away, before she broke down. She could feel Ramon staring after her.

'What do you care?' she thought she heard him call.

She ignored him.

Even exhausted as she was, she barely slept. Turning this way and that, she managed to corkscrew the sleeping bag round her. And every time she heard a step on the duckboards she came up on one elbow, hoping against hope that it was Jack.

Ramon was right, she thought feverishly. Jack was nothing to do with her. He had made that plain enough. She was living in a fantasy world if she pretended anything else.

Even so, she could not help lying on that hard, narrow bed waiting, *waiting...*

It was like a fever. Every sort of feeling banged about in her blood: anticipation; fear for Jack's safety; *need*. It shocked her, shamed her to the heart. But that was what it was all right. The need for Jack's touch, his voice, his simple presence. She needed it like she needed air and water; more, she thought with brave self-mockery, than she seemed to need food.

'Heaven help me,' she said aloud, shaken.

She sat bolt upright in the cold little tent, hugging her knees, and thought about it. In the end she knew there was only one answer.

'I've got to get out of here. I'll tell him as soon as he gets back.'

And he got back, covered in mud and outrageously cheerful, at noon the next day. It seemed like hours before she could get him on his own.

'I shouldn't have come,' she blurted out. 'It's not working out. I have to leave.'

He did not say—as he very reasonably could have done—that she had hardly given it a fair trial. He paused in the act of towelling his hair.

'What brought you to that conclusion?' he asked at last, carefully.

He had just returned from the shower, bare-chested and still damp. The tanned skin gleamed over compact and powerful muscles. He had not shaved. His whole body spoke of primal vitality.

Holly felt a clutch in her stomach. It was becoming all too familiar. To disguise it she said, 'How come you get to wash your hair when I'm not allowed to?'

Jack blinked. A look of unholy amusement came into his eyes. 'Did you *see* me when I got back?'

Oh, yes, she had seen him. Seen and not touched and longed to go to him.

'Yes,' she said curtly.

'Then there's your answer. I was a walking health hazard until I showered. Whereas if you wash all that hair of yours...' his voice deepened noticeably '...all you're doing is using up water to make yourself gorgeous.'

There was a look in his eyes which made her skin prickle. Hurriedly she looked away.

'I don't have a role here,' she said, going back to her original point.

The amusement died out of his eyes.

'That's not what the others say.'

'Oh, I found stuff to do. That's different.'

Jack threw the towel at the tent wall. The angry little movement was in sharp contrast to his level tone when he said, 'It was stuff that needed doing.'

Holly shrugged. 'I still feel I'm here under false pretences.'

'Are you saying you don't feel useful?' Jack was scornful.

This was horrible. She was so wretched that she forgot not to look at him.

'All these people think I'm your *wife*.'

He went very still. 'Ah.'

She glared at him with hot eyes. 'And we both know I'm not.'

'Legally...'

She looked round the bare tent eloquently. 'Legal fictions don't mean much here, do they?'

Jack said on a note of discovery, 'You regret it.'

She had no answer for that at all. She turned away with a helpless gesture.

He said nothing for a moment. Then, utterly expressionless, he said, 'When do you want to go?'

'As soon as possible.' Holly's voice was muffled.

'I'll arrange it.' He paused. 'Where do you want to go? What will you do?'

She had no answer for that either. She had not thought of anything except getting away from his tormenting presence. Jack sighed.

'Don't tell me if you don't want to. Just remember we'll need to stay in touch until we are legally free.'

'Of course,' she said through stiff lips.

She felt as if her heart was shattered ice, with blood seeping out of the cracks.

'OK. I'll get onto it at once but it may take a couple of days.'

A couple of days? How will I bear it?

Her reaction must have shown in her face. He gave a bleak smile.

'Don't worry. You won't see much of me. I have too much work to do.'

It sounded like a death knell.

CHAPTER SEVEN

JACK was as good as his word. Holly did not see him for the rest of the day. It was very late when he came to their tent, but as soon as he detected that she was still awake he collected his laptop computer and went away. The next time she heard the flap she did not make the mistake of stirring so much as a muscle.

It was agony to lie there listening to him take off his clothes. Was it only three nights ago that they had first gone mad in each other's arms?

It was crazy, she thought. They were husband and wife and yet they were as careful of each other as strangers.

But, Holly reminded herself, ten days ago that was exactly what they had been. Strangers. People who did not know each other's names. People with nothing in common. If it had not been for Brendan attacking her, Jack would never even have noticed her.

Except she remembered that first angry encounter—she staggering under her delivery boxes; Jack concentrating on his work and Ramon's self-recriminations. Yet, in spite of their

194

preoccupations, they had looked at each other in that over-lit corridor and recognised *something*. Surely it was not all her imagination?

Her head throbbed with thinking. Long after Jack's breathing had eased into the low rhythm of sleep, Holly lay staring into the darkness. She thought she was trying to explain the past. Or even foresee the future. But in the end she knew that all she was doing was lying there, cradling the unsatisfactory present to her.

These were precious moments, Holly thought, dry-eyed and aching. Tonight she had the right of a wife. Well, half-wife. Tomorrow, or the next day, she would not be able to lie shielded by the dark, sensing that golden chest rise and fall in quiet sleep. Tomorrow or the next day she would be alone again.

She slept at last. Her dreams were bleak.

Jack was not there when she awoke. Of course. But at least today there was no chilly note on his bed.

As soon as she got out into the camp she saw why. Blue-black hair gleaming in the early sun, Jack was striding purposefully towards an arriving convoy. He was wearing creased shorts and an old T-shirt but he still looked as if he ran the world. His long muscular legs moved like oiled pistons and shone like gold.

Holly's heart leaped, then sank like a stone. He looked tough and preoccupied. Not like a man married only three days. Not a man who had just left his new wife sleeping.

He doesn't look like a married man because he doesn't feel like a married man. Never forget that.

He stopped beside the leading truck. A soldier in combat gear leaned out of the cab. Jack ran beside the moving vehicle, clearly giving directions. The soldier nodded and Jack pulled away as the truck accelerated up the dusty track.

Holly realised that he had registered her watching him. It was odd: like being caught out in something shameful. She forced herself to ignore the feeling and smiled at him as best she could.

Their eyes met. Holly found she was holding her breath. But all that happened was that Jack gave her a polite nod. His expression was entirely neutral.

Holly hesitated. Then went over to him.

'Good morning,' he said.

He did not kiss her or put his arm around her. Another truck heaved up the track to them. He waved at the driver and called out in bad Spanish, 'Leave the stuff by the main tent under a tarpaulin.'

'What stuff?' said Holly, as the truck drove on.

'The raw material for a water-powered generator,' said Jack with satisfaction. 'I found a very nice little waterfall yesterday.'

He turned and began to walk towards the main tent. Holly fell into step beside him. After all, she reasoned, he had not actually told her to get lost.

'If they have a waterfall, why isn't there power here already?'

Jack raised his eyebrows as if she surprised him. 'Good point. It's a new waterfall. Formed by the landslides.'

'It sounds very temporary.' And dangerous, though she did not say that.

'That's why I wanted a second opinion yesterday. The geologists say it's stable enough for our purposes. If I can give this place power even for the next few weeks, it will help.'

'*You* can give them?' Holly said uneasily.

'My idea. My design. So I get to build the Lego.' He was clearly exhilarated at the prospect.

She looked up the ruined street. Mud had dried on the buildings, leaving them a uniform red-brown. They looked like a structure fashioned out of chocolate—and about as likely to melt. Behind them the mountains looked enormous but somehow no more solid. Holly shivered.

'How stable is ''stable enough''?'

Jack glanced down at her in surprise. 'Worried about me? There's no need.'

'Of course not,' snapped Holly, recoiling from the suggestion as if she had seen a snake.

They had reached the main tent. He hesitated.

'If you really want to go, you can catch a ride out of here with those guys,' he said, nodding to the army trucks.

'Oh.'

He waited but she did not say anything else. Her thoughts were in too much of a turmoil.

He sighed. 'Well, think about it and let me know. I can get the office to book you a flight to wherever you want to go.'

He can't wait to get rid of me.

'Thank you,' she said in a stifled voice.

'Any time.'

But he didn't look as relaxed as he sounded. There was a little muscle throbbing in his jaw and he pointedly drew back so as not to touch her when she went through the narrow entrance to the tent.

Holly registered signs of disturbance and was marginally encouraged. She turned to him. 'Jack—'

But they were interrupted.

'Oh, there you are, Jack.' It was one of the liaison officers. He had a cold and looked drained.

'What's this about you going back up the mountain today?'

Jack was brisk. 'I've identified a site. The guys and I will put the emergency generator up today.'

The liaison officer was brisker. 'Not today. The army haven't brought an interpreter and I haven't got anyone.'

Jack assimilated this. 'Free one up. This is priority one.'

He made for the coffee urn. The liaison officer gave an exasperated sneeze and pattered after him.

'You're not listening to me, Jack. I haven't got anyone. The nearest qualified interpreter is ten miles and two thousand feet away.'

Jack drew a mug full of sludgy coffee and drank it down as if it was life-giving elixir.

'What about Angelina? I thought she was up here for the duration.'

'With the medical team. And I'm not pulling her out.'

Jack frowned but he seemed to see the justice of that. 'Well, we'll just have to yell at each other. They'll get the idea eventually.'

The liaison officer looked aghast. 'You're crazy. It's dangerous enough without you yelling orders at them in a language they don't understand.'

'Er—maybe I could help,' offered Holly.

The liaison officer turned to her with dawning hope but Jack's frown deepened until his eyebrows met over his nose.

'Out of the question,' he said curtly.

Holly bridled. 'I may not be a professional interpreter but my Spanish is better than yours. By miles.'

'That's not the point.'

'OK. What is the point?'

'It's difficult terrain.'

She looked at him limpidly. He glared at the liaison officer.

'She doesn't know what it's like up there.' He turned back to her. 'You haven't got the right gear. You're not technically qualified.'

Holly still said nothing.

Jack ground his teeth. 'Believe me, you're not prepared.'

'Worried about me?' Holly quoted maliciously. 'There's no need.'

Jack's eyes narrowed to slits.

The liaison officer said swiftly, 'That's great. There you are, Jack. Problem solved.' He gave him a friendly buffet to the shoulder. 'All you've got to do now is talk the army into it.'

Jaw tight, Jack said, 'The weather's too uncertain.'

They both stared at him in disbelief.

Holly said, 'I thought that was why we were here in the first place.'

'Me,' said Jack swiftly. 'Why I am here. You never signed up for dangerous sports.'

Holly met his eyes. She wondered if she was mad. 'For better, for worse. That's what I signed up for, if you remember.'

He was silenced.

'Well, I'm glad that's settled,' the liaison officer murmured.

He faded tactfully. Neither of them noticed.

Jack said, 'But you wanted to leave.'

Holly transferred her gaze to his left ear. 'Still do. But I can make myself useful until I go.'

He stopped arguing. 'Very well. Just get yourself a good breakfast. It's going to be a hard day.'

It was.

Holly realised that she had never seen Jack at work before. She was impressed. If she had thought about it she would have said that he would be dictatorial in the extreme. She would have been wrong.

He was friendly, even relaxed. But he was very, *very* focused. As they toiled up the steep valley, he talked to the soldiers direct so they could laugh at his bad Spanish. But as soon as they reached the waterfall, and precise instructions became important, he slipped seamlessly into using her translation skills.

Holly soon found that he drove the team as mercilessly as he drove himself. They took only the briefest breaks for coffee or high-energy cereal bars. But he did not let them sit and eat, although Holly knew they had food packs and flasks with them.

Yet no one complained. No one except her even seemed to notice. As the soldiers came to the end of one task, Jack outlined the next, illustrating exactly how far it took them towards their goal. They sweated and breathed hard but the soldiers stayed cheerful and the little installation took rapid shape.

'Clever,' said Holly as he dispatched her to the wiring party.

Jack's eyes rested on her unemotionally. Throughout the exercise he had treated her with utter professionalism. You would not have thought there was any relationship between them at all, let alone that they were husband and wife.

Now he shrugged. 'It's what I'm paid for.'

She paused, obscurely irritated. 'Doesn't anyone ever see through all that charm? You've made those guys work like slaves.'

'I've helped those guys achieve a phenomenal result,' he corrected. 'They will be proud of this for the rest of their lives. If it works,' he added under his breath.

Holly was shocked. She had not, she realised, doubted his ability to achieve the goal he set himself. 'What? You mean you're not sure?'

'Not a hundred per cent. That's not for passing on.'

'Of course not,' she said impatiently. 'But you've demanded a hell of a lot from those people if you're only playing the odds.'

Jack looked at her for a long moment. 'You play the odds or you accept failure,' he said quietly. 'That's the choice.'

She looked at him sharply. Was he only talking about the half-built generator?

His eyes glinted unreadably in the thin, hot sun.

'And I always demand a hell of a lot,' he said softly. 'Now get going.'

She did not challenge him again.

Eventually he summoned the soldiers and told them to go back to Ignaz.

'That's it. All we've got to do now is see if it works. See you all later.'

'I'm staying,' said Holly.

He looked at the sky. Low, black clouds were coming in fast.

'I wouldn't advise it. There's going to be the mother of all storms.'

'I'm staying.'

Jack took one look at the set of her chin and did not bother to argue further. But when the soldiers had taken off, their weariness showing at last, he turned back to his installation before they were out of sight.

'Have you ever been in a tropical storm?' he asked over his shoulder.

'No.'

'Think power shower and double it.' He leaned over the edge of the river bank and adjusted the position of one of the rods. 'I'm aiming to get us back to Ignaz before it breaks if I can. But you'd better see if you can find some shelter in case I can't.'

Holly was as tired as the soldiers. But she did not say so. It was a matter of pride. Jack was stripped to the waist and she could see his muscles bunch and strain, bunch and relax, as he struggled with the collector rods. If he could keep going, so could she!

It was just as well she did. There was an ominous note in the wind. By the time she went back to tell Jack that she had found a cave, the clouds were racing like video tape on fast-forward and mud-caked branches were rocking.

'Up there,' she told him, nodding to the head of the waterfall.

Fat drops pancaked onto her bare arm, making her jump. Jack assessed the situation rapidly. He did not waste words. He gathered his equipment with swift economy, zipped it into a waterproof knapsack, and shouldered into it.

'Show me.'

'It's a bit of a scramble.'

Holly led the way. She was so tired now her joints were beginning to burn. She hauled herself along wearily, going onto all fours in the steeper parts. Even with his burden, Jack was tireless. As soon as he saw the cave mouth he pushed past and reached down to help her.

Holly took his offered hand thankfully. He was half supporting her by the time they got into the dark cave.

The wind rumbled louder. She shivered. And then there was a crack like a shattering window and the muddy hillside disappeared behind a sheet of water. Holly stared in disbelief.

'Just in time,' said Jack cheerfully. He unloaded his pack.

'It's like being behind that waterfall,' she said blankly.

'Told you. Power shower times two.'

'You mean this is normal? Not the start of a hurricane or something?'

'We're not in hurricane country,' he said comfortingly. 'It's spectacular but it will pass. We just sit it out. Tell each other our life stories and wait for the sun.'

'Oh.'

It sounded more dangerous even than the water chute outside. She sank down onto the cave floor and leaned against the wall, not answering.

Jack gave her a shrewd look. He extracted the unopened coffee flask from his pack, poured a slug into the tin lid and offered it to her.

Holly took it. She grimaced at the heavily sugared taste but its warmth was reviving. She returned the tin measure to him and tipped her head back wearily.

He poured coffee for himself and slid down beside her. The cave was not cold but the heat seemed to come off his naked torso in waves. Holly tensed.

'Hadn't you better put your shirt on now?'

'Why? I'm not cold.'

In the semi-dark, she felt rather than saw him grin. It was just like their wedding night. Outside the elements thundered, only now it was rain not the steady sensuous beat of the sea on the shore. But inside it was the same, exactly the same—the hammer blows of their heartbeats. And Jack, amused and in control. Just as he was now.

'That's because you've been exercising,' Holly said, inspired. 'Now you've stopped you should cover up.'

He stretched lazily. 'My shirt's in the bottom of the bag.'

His bare shoulder brushed against her as he lowered his arms. Holly set her teeth and refused to react.

'Right,' she said grimly. 'Our life stories. I was born in London. Only child. My mother was my father's long-time lover and didn't tell him about me.'

He made a small sound of surprise and turned towards her. Holly felt the hardness of bone and sinew in the movement, and realised, with a little shiver of strangeness, exactly how strong he was. She drew away infinitesimally and went on with her story.

'Then she died and left me to him as a sort of legacy. He took me back to the States—did I say he was American?'

'Smallville,' he murmured. 'I remember.'

'He had an adopted daughter by his first marriage. She found it difficult but she— Well, she tried. Her husband, on the other hand, was scared out of his mind. He thought I was going to hijack the family company, especially after Dennis died.'

'Dennis?'

'My father. I could never manage to call him "Father". He said he understood.'

'Ah.' He shifted. 'My father always expected met to call him "sir",' he said drily.

She was taken aback. 'You're not serious.'

He shrugged, dismissing it. 'So what happened when your father died?'

The sexy warmth of smooth golden shoulder was so close that she only had to droop her head a little and she could rest against him. The temptation was almost irresistible. Almost.

She said, distracted, 'Dennis left me the company. I was his only family, you see. Oh, Brendan and Donna got the real estate and other stuff, but I got the big potatoes. In trust until I was twenty-five or got married. That's when Brendan got really scared. He tried to marry me off to the man he had brought in to run the company. Homer. Homer Whittard. He was some sort of cousin of Brendan's.'

'I begin to understand,' said Jack slowly.

'I tried to wriggle out of it. I got so desperate I even tried to give the company to Donna and Brendan. It was hopeless. No lawyer would touch me.'

'Of course not.'

Holly was indignant. She forgot the temptations of the broad shoulder and swung round on him, pugnacious.

'Why *of course*?'

'It wouldn't have been very ethical for them to help you to get rid of your inheritance while you were still under age, would it?'

'*Ethical*?' Holly wriggled her shoulders in disgust.

He said in an odd voice, 'You're so young.'

That annoyed her all over again.

'No, I'm not. I've been taking care of myself for years.'

'Have you?'

Her chin came up in pure reflex. 'Yes, I have. Quite successfully, as it happens.'

'It didn't look like that in Paris.'

'You know nothing about it,' she flung at him.

He was utterly still. She suddenly thought: *He's furious!*

'Don't I? I know you were terrified to face Brendan. That you wouldn't even write to your family unless I married you.'

It echoed round the stone walls of the cave like a drum. *Marry you…marry you…marry you…*

Their eyes met. Even in the half-dark she could see the tension in his body.

Marry you…marry you…marry you…

Holly looked away, shaken. 'I never asked you to,' she muttered after a moment.

His reply was quiet. Deadly quiet.

'Didn't you?'

'What do you mean?'

Somehow she had managed to back herself into the rock face. He did not move. But she could feel the heat of his body, his breath. He was breathing unevenly, as he had not done all through the day's physical labour. It seemed as if his body had suddenly remembered that he had climbed a mountain to reach thin and dangerous air. *Why?*

He did not answer her question. Or not the one she asked aloud.

Instead he said softly, 'How did we come to this?'

Holly did not understand. She did not want to understand. Looking anywhere but at Jack, she shook her head violently.

'I don't know what you're talking about.'

'Yes, you do.'

Suddenly there was no longer humid air between their bodies. Unfairly, he took her chin in his hand and forced her to meet his eyes.

'What?' she said goaded.

'Marriage was your only way out, right?'

There was no doubt at all now. He was furious. Holly was so bewildered she forgot to answer. There was a muscle leaping in his jaw and his eyes were black.

'Any man would have done, wouldn't he?'

Holly blinked. *'No!'*

But he swept on, not listening. 'I'm just the guy who drew the short straw. Again. Oh, God, how do I get myself into these things?'

Again? Holly did not understand. But somehow she knew it was important to tell the truth about this.

'Any man *wouldn't* do,' she said hotly. 'Nobody else—'

But the look he turned on her stopped the words in her mouth.

'J-Jack?' she said uncertainly.

'Oh, it's me you want, is it?' It seemed to make him even angrier. 'You sure about that?'

And before she knew what he was doing, he had taken her face between powerful hands and was kissing her. Hard.

Oh, God, it was devastatingly familiar. And so *right.*

He was so confident; so horribly, justifiably confident. Holly felt as if his every movement was wired into her own circuits. On the one hand this man was a stranger—an impatient, driven stranger. Yet at the same time he already knew almost more about her than she did herself. Certainly he knew how to drive her responses to the very edge. And he was her husband!

She screwed her eyes tight shut and struggled to make sense of it all. Or that was what she told herself as her pulse pounded and her body shook to its core.

Jack made a small sound of satisfaction. His hands, those long, deft hands, moved with total assurance. She felt herself tipping, slipping sideways, stretching her length along the stony floor.

There was a palm under her T-shirt, between her shoulderblades; another, possessive, at her hip. He pressed her to the ground. His smooth golden chest was hot as a furnace. Holly's lips parted in a breath of pure desire. And all the time his mouth teased and promised and lured until Holly's senses swam.

'What do you want?' His voice was uneven.

I want you to love me.

She had no idea where the voice in her head had come from. It terrified her. She froze.

Jack felt it. He raised his head and looked down at her.

'*Tell* me,' he said urgently.

But she just stared at him, too shaken by the revelation she had just experienced to speak.

I'm in love with him. That's why the marriage service seemed so real. That's why we made love. That's why I haven't slept properly since. I love Jack Armour.

He lifted himself and took hold of her T-shirt to pull it over her head. Still stunned, Holly raised her hands like a puppet.

'Stop it,' said Jack furiously. 'You're not a child.'

She blinked, stung. 'Wh-what?'

'Don't go limp and pliant on me. If you want me, have the guts to show me.'

'Want you?' Holly was outraged that he did not already know. '*Want* you?'

She thrust him away and struggled up onto an elbow. Turned. Pushed him to the ground. Saw his eyes flare in the dark.

He gave a ragged laugh. 'Show me, then.' And let his hands fall.

She knew he would not touch her again unless she made him. Half-angry, half-determined, Holly set herself to test his resistance to breaking point. She folded herself over him, savouring the smell of his skin, stroking the long athlete's limbs, tasting him. She felt him grit his teeth as her tongue-tip explored.

'Holly,' he groaned.

She smiled against his skin. He shuddered uncontrollably as she found the hollow of his hip bone.

'Holly, for God's sake!'

Suddenly it seemed he could not stand any more. His hands no longer lay determinedly idle. He tipped her onto her back. Holly gave herself up to the senses. In sheer rapturous excitement, she forgot all restraint. It was magic. It was what she was born for. Jack was *hers*.

Only he wasn't.

With a great cry of despair, she thrust him away and leaped to her feet.

'*No,*' she shouted. It was savage.

Jack got up. He turned her to face him, his hands warm against the shivering skin of her shoulders.

'Hol?'

She shook herself free. She would not met his eyes. 'I'm cold.'

He gave a soft, sexy laugh. 'No, you're not.'

For a moment Holly almost hated him. 'Yes, I am,' she shouted. 'And you're not helping. For heaven's sake, get dressed.'

He scanned her face. She could sense his bewilderment, to say nothing of his frustration, and there was not a thing she could do about it.

In the end he let her go with a sigh.

'Your shirt.' He gave it to her, then went over to his pack and hauled things out of it until he found his own. 'My shirt.' He pulled it on with jerky movements. 'Better?' he said with savage mockery.

Holly huddled into her T-shirt. Then she sat down against the cave wall and hugged her knees. Her legs were trembling. She did not answer.

With a little exclamation of disgust, Jack went to the mouth of the cave. The landscape was still obscured by a silver curtain of water. Wind and water roared around the mountain side like a wild beast. But not loudly enough to drown her kettle-drum of a heart.

I love him. I love him.

She looked at him as he stood there, dark against the rain. He had his back to her, his head half turned to look down the valley. He was tall as a warrior, dark and deadly as a Barbary pirate. He looked whipcord-thin but she knew—didn't she?—the strength in that sleek body.

And I love him. I love him.

She hauled herself to her feet and went over to him.

Without looking at her, he said, 'If you were always going to end up with a marriage of convenience, it would have saved a lot of time if you'd stuck with the guy in Smallville.'

Holly flinched. But she also thought she heard a touch of hurt in his voice. She had never been so uncertain of what she wanted but she knew she could not bear to have hurt Jack.

'It's not the same thing at all.'

'Isn't it? Explain the difference to me.'

She struggled to put it into words. 'You were thinking about me. Not your career or the company. Me.'

'How do you know the other guy wasn't?'

'Homer?' She was so startled she laughed aloud. 'It was obvious. All he cared about was getting his hands on a stake in the business. I knew that.'

'Yes, but you're not very good at reading men,' Jack said quietly.

It was like a blow. Holly took a step backwards.

'That's not fair.'

He swung round. He did not touch her. Repressed anger vibrated off him like sound waves.

'You can't just—'

But Holly did not let him finish. 'I know what this is about,' she spat. 'Virginity was a bad mistake, wasn't it?'

For a moment Jack looked absolutely murderous.

She went on recklessly, 'Well, if I'd realised it was going to be such a problem, I'd have unloaded before.'

He was as pale as the golden skin permitted. 'Why didn't you?' The taut mouth barely moved.

'Because I never wanted to,' Holly yelled.

'Why not?'

It was a question she had asked herself. All the fight went out of her.

'Oh, who knows?' she said wearily. 'Maybe I was too suspicious of guys who seemed to be attracted to me. Maybe I wasn't in one place long enough.' She hesitated. 'Maybe there's something wrong with me.'

There was a long, complicated silence.

Then—'There's nothing wrong with you,' he said curtly.

He still did not touch her. But something gave her hope. She moved closer.

'Isn't there?'

'No.'

'Then why do you say I can't read men?'

'Because—' he began in a goaded tone. Then stopped dead. He folded his lips together as if they would never open again.

Holly took another step forward.

'It's because I'm not sophisticated enough, isn't it? Is that why you didn't tell me about Susana?'

His eyes flared. 'How do you know about Susana?'

'Oh, someone usually tells the wife about the mistress,' she said, demonstrating her sophistication.

'What?'

'Did you think I wouldn't find out?'

He shook his head helplessly. 'I didn't think it was anything to do with you.'

It went in like a stiletto: so true you hardly felt it; so deadly you began to bleed to death.

Holly kept her smile steady, though she could feel the cold spreading from her heart. It was all too familiar. After her mother died, ice floes had locked her into place for years, getting her through the tensions of the house in Lansing Mills and the loss of everything she knew. She had prayed she would never feel like that again.

She said, almost in desperation, 'Even after I became your wife?'

'Not a wife in that way.'

'In every way there is,' Holly pointed out, still smiling.

It was Jack's turn to flinch. He said hurriedly, 'What did they tell you about Susana?'

'That she was the love of your life. Were they wrong?'

He closed his eyes briefly. 'No.'

The hot rain thundered outside but Holly was cold to her fingertips.

'So when you married me you...?'

'I was trying to help. All right? That's all.'

'And when you made love to me?'

'Come on,' he said harshly. 'You can't read men that badly. I wanted you.'

The cold was like a pain. All she wanted was for him to hold her. Even if he did not love her. Even if he despised her.

She said softly, 'So you don't want me any more?'

He pushed an agitated hand through his hair. 'Don't play games you don't want to finish.'

'And if I've changed my mind? If I do want to finish them?'

He went very still.

She took the final step. 'I'm your wife. I want to feel like your wife.'

She put a hand on his chest. Under the shirt she could feel his heart was racing. She pressed herself against him. For a moment he stood like a rock. Only that sprinting heart betrayed him.

She put up both hands. His smooth dark hair was still damp, soft as an animal's pelt, under her fingers. She brought his head down to meet her kiss.

He groaned. But his groan was lost in her mouth.

The rain pounded on the rocks outside. In the humid cave they were as alone as the last man and woman on earth. Or the first.

Holly was terrified. She was jubilant. She was on a journey she had never made before. Unashamed, she tore at his clothes. Naked in her arms he was slim and muscular. And out of control.

He made her writhe. He made her growl with pleasure. He made her scream until the cave bounced with the sound. And then, shatteringly, he exploded deep, deep inside her, blasting away the ice for ever.

It was only afterwards, when they lay spent on the rough cave floor, that he broke her heart.

Stretching lazily, he murmured, 'Do you feel like my wife now?'

Heaven help her, he sounded kind but quite, quite detached. And hc did not say that he felt like her husband.

CHAPTER EIGHT

A WEEK later Holly was sitting in a lawyer's office in London.

'This is a mess,' said the man on the other side of the big desk. He frowned.

Holly remembered that frown. He had been her mother's lawyer. It was he who had taken her to the Dorchester to meet her American father for the first time. And it was he who had broken the news that Dennis was taking her back to Lansing Mills with him and there was nothing anyone could do to stop him.

He had been sympathetic but firm then. He was the same now, all these years later.

'First of all, how are you managing? London must seem strange after all this time.'

Holly smiled wanly. 'Not a problem. Surviving in strange cities is what I do.'

He looked faintly alarmed.

She took pity on him. 'I've got a room and I've signed on with an agency to do cleaning. It will do while I take stock.'

He was relieved but disapproving. 'That's not necessary. I can advance you money from your mother's estate…'

Holly bit her lip. 'Jack gave me enough money to tide me over.'

There was a little silence. 'Ah, yes. Mr Armour.'

She looked down at her hands.

'My assistant has been in touch with his firm in Miami. They seem to be in regular communication with him. He has expressed a wish that you stay in his house in Shropshire until your legal situation is clarified. I believe you have been there?'

'Yes,' said Holly. Her lips felt numb. 'When we first left France.'

The cold, empty house had appalled her. Now, of course, she knew why it was so empty. He had bought it for the love of his life, only she had not wanted it in the end.

'Good,' said the lawyer, oblivious.

'But I don't want to stay there.'

He took off his glasses and sat back in his chair. 'I can understand that. It seems rather isolated. If you're afraid, I am empowered to arrange for a housekeeper to live with you.'

Holly was offended. 'I'm not afraid. I just don't want to live in—in someone else's house.'

'I appreciate that. Nevertheless, from my point of view it would be a great deal easier if you could bring yourself to do it. Just until the dispositions under your father's will are resolved.'

'Why?' she said, preparing for battle.

He rounded up a trail of paper clips across his blotter.

'Your father was—how shall I put this?—determined to have his own way. Well, look at the way he changed your name and got you an American passport as well as your English one. You withheld your consent but it made no difference.'

'He rode roughshod over everyone,' said Holly. 'Not just me.'

'Quite. That included his lawyers, I imagine. That will is crazy. But it is there and you've got a brother in law who is going to use any means he can to retain full control of your inheritance. So we mustn't give him any. Do you understand?'

'No.'

He stopped playing with the paper clips. 'All right. Put it this way. I've sent off your marriage certificate to the Lansing lawyers. That should release your inheritance. But I've already had notification that they intend to challenge it on the grounds that it is just a legal fiction.'

Holly was appalled. That possibility had never occurred to her.

'Can they do that?'

'They can do anything Brendan Sugrue tells them to do. I can go to court and defend it, of course. We'd probably win in the end. Meanwhile, you're probably talking two sets of American lawyers, a lot of time, the risk that there could be an order requiring you to live with the Sugrues again... The possible complications are endless.'

Holly closed her eyes. 'Why are they doing this to me?'

'Money.'

'What?'

'I don't think you realise quite how wealthy your father was,' the lawyer told her drily.

Holly opened her eyes and stared. 'Well, the house was huge in comparison with my mother's flat, but—'

'Your father,' said the lawyer deliberately, 'ran a multinational empire. By the time he died his personal assets amounted to hundreds of millions of dollars. That's why it's worth Brendan Sugrue fighting to keep you under his guardianship. That's why lawyers will take it, no matter how weak the underlying case.'

'Hundred of millions?' Holly could not take it in.

'That's how he met your mother. She was his secretary, running his European private office. They had an affair whenever he was over.'

Holly remembered her mother's sadness. At last it made sense. 'I see.'

'I suspect,' said the lawyer, suddenly unprofessional, 'that when he found out about you he was shocked that she had managed to do something without taking his orders about it. Oh, he took his responsibility to you seriously, no doubt about that. But he was also reasserting his right to dominate. I imagine that's what that crazy will is all about.'

'Makes sense,' said Holly absently. '*Hundreds* of millions?'

'Most of it goes to his charitable foundation, but there's still plenty left for you and your sister. You will be a wealthy woman.'

'I don't want—' said Holly, revolted. And stopped. She remembered Jack saying ruefully, 'What we need is a friendly millionaire.'

'We can all think of something we would do with a few million dollars,' the lawyer said understandingly. 'So you don't want to blow half of it on law suits. My best advice is take Mr

Armour's offer and carry on as his wife while I sort this out.'

A friendly millionaire. She had seen his passionate commitment and the work that Armour Disaster Recovery could do. It would be a good use of the money, Holly thought. And it would go some way to paying her debt to Jack. Maybe then she would have a chance of forgetting him.

'All right,' she said, accepting the inevitable.

The lawyer gave a sigh of relief. He became brisk.

'Right. No more cleaning jobs. You pick up the keys from Armour's London office. Here's the address. You will need a bank account, credit cards. Give them my name as a reference. Meanwhile I'll arrange a cash advance for you.'

Holly felt slightly overwhelmed. 'Th-thank you.'

'I suggest you go down to Shropshire as soon as possible. Then when Sugrue's agents start investigating, they will find that you are living in your husband's house.'

That hurt.

'Yes,' said Holly woodenly.

'There's a train with reasonable connections this afternoon. Of course, in a lonely place like that you'll need a car.' A thought occurred to him. 'I suppose you do drive?'

'No. I've never stayed anywhere long enough—or had enough money—to learn.'

He beamed. 'Well, you can take lessons while you're waiting.'

'Waiting for what?' said Holly suddenly suspicious.

For the first time he looked uncomfortable. 'For your inheritance to be transferred, of course.'

She looked at him narrowly. He would not meet her eyes, shifting in his chair and pushing the paper clips about distractedly.

'It will all work out,' he muttered. 'I'm sure.'

Holly was still turning that remark over in her mind when she let herself in to Jack's house that evening. It was only one oddity in an all-round strange day but for some reason it disturbed her more than the other things. More even than the fact that the people at Armour's London office had expected her, had been delighted to see her and had passed on messages from Jack just as if it was an ordinary marriage.

It all seemed too pat, somehow. Too contrived. As if Jack was sitting somewhere behind a curtain taking control of her life again.

'Paranoia,' she said aloud. 'Jack's got more important things to think about than me. I'm not the love of his life, after all.'

She kept reminding herself of that as she reacquainted herself with the house he had brought her to so briefly. With a little smile, Holly remembered what a shock the house had been. For one thing, it was more of a castle than a house. For another, it was in the middle of nowhere. For a third, it was empty.

Holly remembered how totally she had known it was empty as soon as they walked in through the front door. Oh, it was tidy and polished— someone obviously came in to clean—but the coldness hit her. And the echoes. Their footsteps reverberated as if they were in an underground cavern.

This is a house that has not been lived in for a long time, she had thought. In fact it felt as if no one had ever lived there. She had looked round the empty walls and wondered *why*.

Now, of course, she knew. He had bought it for Susana. And she had never lived there.

Now Holly surveyed the high-ceilinged hall ironically. She had even wondered if it was some inherited pile. She remembered asking him.

He had grinned. Oh, how she loved that look, when his eyes danced. 'Not me. I'm a thorough mongrel. My mother was Ecuadorean, my father American military. But when you get to my grandparents and beyond it's real soup.'

She had laughed. She had been beginning to think they would be friends. And her instincts, though she had not realised it, had been beginning to tell her they would be a great deal more than friends.

'And how many of them were medieval barons?' she had teased him.

He had laughed and led her into what was clearly a drawing room of sorts. Holly wandered there now. It looked the same. She could almost feel his warm presence at her shoulder.

There were brilliant-coloured rugs on the floor but they could not completely hide the grey stone flags underneath. Add to that a couple of tall-backed Jacobean chairs, their wood black with age, and a fireplace big enough to roast an ox in, and you had a seriously antique ambience. Cold, under-furnished and inhuman; but as authentic as a museum.

It had seemed odd then and it still seemed odd now. Nothing she knew of Jack—and she knew him pretty well by now, Holly thought drily—suggested he would enjoy this arid magnificence. Or that he would fall unalterably in love with a woman who would.

'Of course, he's not exactly into cosy,' she reminded herself, as she trailed her old roll bag upstairs.

The bedrooms were not much better. Holly took possession of a four-poster with green velvet hangings. When she pulled back the coverlet, the smell of dust was overpowering. There was blanket chest under the small window and a huge polished cupboard to hang her clothes. But no cushions, no ornaments, no *books*. Even in her Montmartre garret she had made room for her books.

She unzipped her bag and put *Jane Eyre* and *Charlie and the Chocolate Factory* defiantly on the window chest. Bending, she peered out and saw a tangled garden leading down to what was probably a stream under the weeds. Further away, towards the distant hills, there were houses and a church spire, neat as a child's toy, but the garden was a wilderness. In the spring dusk, it was full of shadows.

Holly shivered and drew back. She had lived all her life in the anonymous bustle of cities or Lansing Mills where she could not go to the gas station without people asking after her family or her school results. Isolation was going to be a new experience.

It would be heaven, if only Jack were here too. Why didn't I realise that last time we were here? If only…

Holly gave an exclamation of annoyance. Betrayed by her wayward memory again!

But she could not help it. *If only I had realised I was in love with him then. If only I had told him.*

Abruptly, she turned away from the window and stamped downstairs, furious with herself.

'If only, nothing!' she lectured herself. 'Susana was the love of his life. He told you that. There's nothing you could ever have done about it. Think! He kept telling you how young you are. He just doesn't see you as a woman.'

But he made love to me as a woman. No doubt about that.

Tears pricked Holly's eyes. She dashed them away angrily.

'What's that got to do with it? He doesn't *love* you! Hang on to that, Holly and don't be a fool.'

She made her way into the kitchen. Its size and equipment would have had Chef Pierre dancing with delight but there was a distinct absence of food. The fridge stood empty. The freezer was turned off. The old-fashioned larder offered only a box of candles and some matches. This barrenness made her realise that she had not eaten since she bought a croissant at a city sandwich bar for breakfast.

Last time, Holly remembered, Jack had taken them to a pub to eat. She tried to remember where it was. Of course, last time there had been his rented car. She began to realise why the taxi driver who had brought her from the station had pressed his business card on her. Thank heavens the lawyer had given her all that cash. She was going to need it!

She went out to eat. The landlord recognised her.

Holly was taken aback.

'Only a couple of weeks since the last time,' the man reminded her, putting a substantial plate in front of her. 'You were with your husband. From the castle, isn't it?'

Husband! That was what he had said the last time. And made her feel as if she had fallen off a cliff.

Jack had noticed.

'He called me your husband,' he repeated calmly. 'Which is what I will be in three days' time. You'd better get used to it.'

'But—'

'You can't faint every time somebody refers to our marriage,' he had said crisply. 'It will give the game away. Besides, it's not flattering.'

Holly had shut her eyes. 'I never thought… All of a sudden it seemed so real.'

'It is real,' Jack had said, losing his amusement. 'Unless you want to forget the whole thing?'

Panic brushed its moth wing up her spine. Why, oh why, had she not known *then* that she was falling in love with him?

'No.'

'Then practise saying "my husband Jack" twenty times every morning before breakfast. You'll soon get the hang of it.'

But of course she hadn't. So now, when the expansive landlord said, so casually, 'You were with your husband,' she went cold.

The landlord peered at her. 'You all right, Mrs Armour?'

Mrs Armour! Oh, Lord, how words could turn the knife in the wound. It was as bad as when the Sugar Islanders had called her *the bride*. She hadn't been a bride, not really. Any more than she was really Mrs Armour. And yet… And yet…

She looked down at her rings: the heavy diamond she had not expected and didn't want; the plain gold band. They both felt like props in some play that she did not really want to be in. It was like a nightmare. Except that it was going to take more escaping from than the simple effort of waking. And she could not do a thing about it until the lawyer told her she was free.

She said with an effort, 'I'm fine. Jet-lag catching up with me, I guess.'

Free? Who was she fooling? She was in love with Jack. How did you get free of that? Oh, she could run away again, make sure she never saw him again. It wouldn't make any difference. She would carry this love with her until somehow, please God, it would wear itself out.

She paid the bill and called the village taxi to take her home again.

In the next few weeks she learned to think of the gloomy castle as 'home' indeed. Tentatively at first, then with more assurance, she moved furniture round. She opened the windows, tumbled curtains, bought cushions. Eventually, she applied herself to finding out what was in the garden and what it needed to come back to life.

She opened her bank account, started driving lessons and slowly began to build a life for herself. She found a chamber group who welcomed her flute. She helped out at the village school with reading groups and began to make friends.

Her life was punctuated by supportive phone calls from her lawyer and slightly more distant ones from Jack's London colleagues. Jack himself called once, on a line that broke up badly. The only thing that was clear was his urgency that she should stay in Shropshire.

'Don't worry,' said Holly wryly. 'My lawyer has laid it on the line for me.'

'I'll see you...' But that was when the line broke up terminally.

His office, when she rang them, had no news that he was coming to the UK.

'But since you called, Mrs Armour—'

That name again! Holly was glad that the woman could not see her wince. The London office manager was devastatingly pretty and clearly thought Jack was a hero.

'We've had a request for an interview from *Elegance* magazine. I explained Jack was still away but their columnist said she'd be really interested to meet you. I know Jack saw her in Ignaz—'

It hung in the air.

'I don't know anything about talking to journalists,' protested Holly.

'We'll do the serious briefing here.' In addition to being pretty and star-struck, the office manager was comprehensively patronising.

So it was a matter of pride to agree.

Pride faltered a bit when Rita Caruso arrived, however. Confronted with a frighteningly fashionable brunette, Holly silently cursed her own unwariness. But she put a good face on it and invited the woman to look round.

'What a pile!' said Rita Caruso, pointing her camera at an arched window. 'Haven't been married long, have you?'

'No.'

Rita moved round to the Jacobean table, its dark polish now reflecting a bowl of early roses. Holly had found them struggling through the brambles at the end of the garden and hadn't been able to resist picking a few. They smelled of honey and pepper and long summer evenings and their perfume filled the cool room.

'*Very* nice,' said Rita. 'I hear you were with him at Ignaz for a while. I suppose he shipped you out when the storm warning hit?'

Holly did not say she had no idea there had been a storm warning. Instead she said evasively, 'There was a lot to do here.'

'I can see.'

Rita made her way confidently through the house. Holly followed.

'Been together long?'

'What?'

'You and Jack Armour. God, that man is a hunk!'

'Er—yes,' said Holly disconcerted.

Rita misunderstood her. 'I knew he was too tasty to be on his own, even though he said he didn't have a wife,' she said philosophically. She let her camera fall for a moment, took Holly's arm and walked her out through a French window onto the reclaimed terrace. 'Now, tell me what it's like to be married to a Hercules.'

Holly gave a choke of laughter, quickly suppressed.

'I suppose I don't see him quite like that,' she murmured.

Rita gave her an engaging smile. 'You will. By the time I've finished you will see that devastating husband of yours the way every sane woman sees him.' She gave an eloquent shimmy of pure lust. 'Brrr. Our readers are gonna love it.'

Holly could not dislike her. After all, Holly had fallen for the Gorgeous Jack effect herself, hadn't she?

She said, 'Let me give you some coffee and you can tell me exactly what you want to know. I'll help if I can. But you must realise that I can't betray Jack's confidence.'

'Just tell me how you met and fell in love,' said Rita. 'That'll do it for me.'

'But I thought it was a profile.'

'Yeah, in a way. I'm thinking of a series on men of action. Contrast their work with the private man at home. I thought of it when I saw the stuff I got in Ignaz. Oh boy, you wait till you see those pictures.'

'Has Jack seen them?' Holly asked with misgiving.

Rita shrugged. 'He signed the release,' she said airily. 'This is going to be *hot*.'

So Holly made her coffee and gave her a carefully edited account of their meeting in Paris. Rita drew all the wrong conclusions and was enchanted.

'So you'd only known each other a week when you married? What a *story!* I knew the guy had to be a romantic at heart.'

And she was off. Too late, Holly realised the trap she had walked into. Anything that she said now either sounded coy or betrayed the true nature of their marriage to an interested world. She had an obscure feeling that it would let Jack down, somehow. Quite apart from the fact that it would give Brendan Sugrue exactly the evidence he was no doubt looking for.

The moment Rita Caruso left, she rushed to the bathroom and was violently sick.

She tried to ring Jack to warn him. None of the numbers she had produced any result. So she called the London office.

'I think I ought to speak to him. I talked to that journalist.'

'We know, Mrs Armour,' said the odiously patient office manager, Louise. 'We set it up. I assure you the interview had Jack's approval.'

Holly was desperate. 'But you don't know what I *said*.'

'Don't worry. We did a full technical briefing; that's what's important. Jack won't care about the personal stuff.'

And that, thought Holly, was probably true. It depressed her so much she was sick again.

She flung herself into a fever of gardening. She was outside every morning as soon as the silvery sun was up and stayed there until it was dark. She hacked down layer upon layer of undergrowth to reveal a forest of neglected rose bushes underplanted with lavender. The detritus made several cheering bonfires and the garden began to look like the rose paradise it had clearly been designed to be.

Holly developed muscles she hadn't known she had, an ache in the small of her back and a veritable craving for lemon barley water. Her primary school class came for tea. It became common for cars to make their way up the overgrown drive. She was—nearly—happy.

One perfect evening the music group rehearsed on the mossy lawn. They were pacing through a stately Purcell 'Chaconne' when a car drew up. Quietly, its lone passenger made his way through the vividly untidy house to the terrace.

He stood there unobserved for a moment. In the evening sun the garden was bathed in apricot light. Flowers he had not known were there nodded in the slight breeze. Bees buzzed. The chamber group sawed and blew and nodded through music that spiralled and fell in measured waves. And in the middle, her face absorbed, was Holly.

Jack watched her. She had scooped her hair back untidily and the sun refracted off escaping fronds to turn the harvest-brown into gold lit by rainbows. Her days in the open air had given her a faint golden tan and a dusting of freckles. She wore a skimpy cotton top and an expression of intense concentration. She looked happy.

And very young, he thought. His hand clenched on the door frame until the knuckles showed white.

The 'Chaconne' finished. Jack unclenched his fingers and strolled forward.

'Beautiful.'

Holly looked up. Startled, she gave him a blindingly brilliant smile. He went very still. Her smile died.

For a moment she did not move. Everyone else around her was getting up and greeting him a little nervously, because he had been a formidable absent figure in the village for a long time. But she could not move.

He shook hands with their lead violin and the music group's director.

'I hope you don't mind—' the latter said.

'Not at all. Just the right music for an English garden,' Jack said easily. He watched Holly out of the corner of his eye. 'Idyllic homecoming.'

She seemed to come to herself at that. Carefully she put her flute down on the grass and got up.

'How are you, Jack?' She did not offer to kiss him or come close enough for an embrace. 'I didn't know you were back.'

'Flew in this afternoon. Drove straight here.'

Her eyes lifted swiftly. He caught puzzlement in them before they fell.

'Then you'll be tired. Perhaps we'd better stop.'

'No. Carry on with your rehearsal. I could do with a shower, anyway. Afterwards I'll come and listen if you're still playing.'

But he did not.

They wound up at nine-thirty. Holly, normally the most hospitable hostess, did not offer them coffee and they, understanding, did not delay their departure. She went upstairs, her heart beating hard.

Jack had had his shower; and fallen asleep.

He was face down on the green-hung four-poster, slumbering deeply. He was naked except for a towel round his waist and the window was open. Holly went over softly and closed it.

The sound must have disturbed him. He stirred, murmuring. She went to the bed.

'Yes?' she said softly.

He opened his eyes and stared up at her as if he did not know who she was or where he was.

Holly could not help herself. She reached out and laid her hand against the familiar cheek. It was cool and unexpectedly smooth. He must have shaved, she thought, surprised.

And then he took hold of her hand and pulled her down on top of him. Her senses leaped in answer.

Wordless, he slid his hands under her skirt, moulding her naked thighs with exquisite precision until she writhed restlessly against him. Wordless, she flung off her clothes and kissed the length of his body in feverish longing, heightened by weeks of absence. Fierce and silent, they took hold of each other and drove and tumbled and gripped until he gave a harsh cry and collapsed, still holding her like a vice.

Holly lay panting. Her head whirled. Her body throbbed with a thirst only partly slaked. She was stunned. How could she behave like that? What had happened to her?

Almost at once, Jack fell asleep. Holly made quite certain that he was unconscious before she eased gently out of his embrace. Even in sleep, though, his arms tightened possessively for a moment before she managed to extract herself.

Her legs unsteady, Holly made her way along the hall to the bathroom. She thought she would get fresh linen from the airing cupboard to make up another bed. But when she get there she sank down onto the side of the bath, shaking.

What was wrong with her? She put a hand over her mouth. Her lips were trembling. Her whole body was trembling. She felt weak as water, vulnerable and shattered to the core.

Of course, Jack might not even have known it was her. He had not once called her by her name. He was exhausted, jet-lagged, and the summer dusk was a disguise he might have been glad to be deceived by. Maybe subconsciously he had pretended he was making love to Susana. Maybe even believed it. It had certainly felt like love.

Holly turned and rested her forehead against the cool bathroom tiles. She hurt so much she could not cry. It was as if all the tears had been burned out of her.

She heard a noise and looked up. Jack was standing in the doorway. His body seemed to be poised for something, like a physical question mark. In the full dark he was no more than a shadow but she knew the expression on his face as well as if she had seen it in a spotlight. Horror.

Her body revolted against the pain. With a small cry Holly turned away and was comprehensively sick.

CHAPTER NINE

AND that seemed to answer the question, whatever it was.

Jack slid the robe from the back of the door
round her naked shoulders and waited until she
had finished. Then he wiped her face very gently
with a warm flannel. His hands were quite impersonal.

He took her back to the four-poster. She noticed that the coverlet was smooth. He must have
straightened the tangled bedclothes before he
came to look for her.

The consideration in that simple action moved
Holly oddly. Once again, tears prickled against
her eyelids. She rubbed them away.

'I'm sorry,' she muttered. 'I don't know why
I've started crying all the time. It's not like me.'

'Stress,' he said briefly.

He watched her get into bed without touching
her again. She turned to him.

'Jack, I'm sorry. I mean—earlier.' She was
floundering and the shadowed face did not help
her. 'I never meant—'

She did not know what she meant. Except *I love you. Hold me.* And she couldn't say that. She gave up.

'We both got carried away,' Jack said coolly. 'No harm done.'

It was like a slap in the face.

Holly called on all her reserves of pride. 'I suppose not,' she managed.

He gave a short nod. 'As long as that's understood.' He sent to the door. 'Sleep well. I'll be down the hall if you want me.'

And he was gone.

It was the start of the strangest month in her life. He treated her with friendliness. Sometimes it almost felt like intimacy. He talked about his life, his work, the distant family he hardly saw, the friends he counted on. He even talked over his plans with her—only they never, ever included her. And he never once mentioned Susana.

It must hurt, thought Holly, seeing another woman in the house he had bought for the love of his life. She tried to say as much but he did not—or would not—understand her.

'You've brought the old place to life. Never apologise for that. In fact, I think we should revive the old swimming pool as well, don't you?'

It was the first time that he had suggested anything like a shared project. Holly warmed.

'I didn't know there was one.'

He laughed at her, the dark eyes lighting in the way she loved.

'That's because your excavations haven't got as far as the orchard yet. I'll get a man in to clear it.'

He did. And to Geoff, who drove the digger, and Kevin, his assistant, they must have looked the most united couple, Holly thought. He was unfailingly courteous. More than that, he lavished things on her, encouraging her to buy clothes and books and CDs she would normally have rejected as way beyond her means.

For her part, Holly consulted him on everything, waved him off without complaint when he had to travel, met him with pleasure when he returned.

And they said goodnight, every night, at the top of the stairs.

Holly had never slept so badly or been so jumpy. Her digestion stayed queasy, though she hid it from Jack. He was not in a mood to notice much anyway, she thought. He was concentrating on a report for the Paris committee and treated her with polite detachment.

So outwardly she stayed calm, working long hours in the garden. She continued with her music but the primary school broke up for the summer and that blocked one of her escape routes. Jack persuaded her to go to coffee with the local gentry but that was hard work. The driving lessons used up time and her instructor was soon talking about putting her in for her driving test. It was hard to tell but she thought that Jack was pleased.

He was even polite about the article in *Elegance* when it arrived. Watching anxiously, Holly thought she detected a wince from time to time, presumably when he found the account of their falling in love at first sight.

'I'm sorry. She rather got away from me,' Holly said.

'Don't worry about it. Journalists always have an angle they want to play.' He smiled, but his eyes were unamused. 'At least she's stopped asking for photographs with my kit off.'

'*What?*'

'She turned up at Ignaz and decided I was a Man of Action, God help me. For a time, every other e-mail I got was from her, suggesting themes for a photo shoot. Haute couture interspersed with the odd frolic in a waterfall, from what I remember.'

Holly gulped. She could feel her face heat at the thought. And then remembered something.

'That man we met at the dinner in Paris,' she said. 'You *said* his colleague wanted you to model. I'd forgotten.'

'Of course you did. You didn't believe it. You said, ''Model what? Civil servant chic?''' said Jack. The smile still did not reach his eyes.

Holly blinked. 'I'd forgotten that, too.'

'I hadn't.' He turned another couple of pages. 'You were right.'

'Rita Caruso doesn't think so.'

And nor do I.

'Rita Caruso doesn't let truth get in the way of a good story,' he said drily.

She managed not to wince but it was an effort. Fortunately, he was too absorbed to notice.

'And now I shall be Jack the Romantic until people forget. Let's hope none of the papers pick it up.'

But of course they did. Worse than that, someone, maybe at Brendan Sugrue's instigation, made the connection with missing heiress Holly Lansing. Suddenly Jack was less a romantic hero than a fortune hunter of the worst kind.

'I'm so *sorry*,' said Holly, nearly in tears at a particularly cynical article. The office was sending them press cuttings daily by then.

Jack shrugged. 'Sticks and stones. It will pass.' He considered her frowningly. 'You're looking pale. Is this getting you down? Do you want to come to Paris with me when I deliver my report?'

Holly held her breath. 'Why?'

He hesitated. 'At least that way you wouldn't be alone here if some newspaperman tracks us down to the house.'

'Oh.' She was so disappointed she could have screamed. 'I don't think so, thank you. Running away isn't a great idea. At least, it hasn't done me much good so far. I'm better off staying here.'

She did not look at him. The temptation to fling herself into his arms and beg him to love her was too great.

His face was masklike. 'If that's what you want.'

The silence between them stretched as taut as piano wire.

If only, Holly thought in frustration, he was not so handsome that every lady photojournalist in the western hemisphere wanted to do the same thing! She might have stood a chance. All right, Susana was the love of his life. Holly couldn't fight that. But Jack couldn't mourn her for ever. Eventually he would want—well, second best. A home. Some affection. Holly could give him that. But the trouble was the competition. The world was full of women queuing up to comfort Gorgeous Jack.

Her nails curved into her palms until they hurt. 'I do,' she said with unmistakeable sincerity.

So he went alone.

As soon as he had gone, Holly wished she had answered differently. But then the mail brought the morning's press cuttings and she could only be glad that she did not have to face him. According to a mid-West journalist, clearly briefed by Brendan, Holly had led a life of unbridled excess from the moment she left the family roof.

'Revolting,' she cried, flinging the cuttings away from her. She felt as if something slimy had crawled over her skin.

It upset her enough to put her off breakfast. It even disrupted her normally confident driving lesson.

'Are you all right?' asked her instructor, worried.

'Yes, I'm...'

But she felt so dizzy that she braked to a halt and leaned, white-faced, against the driver's window.

The instructor was a nice man. He was concerned. 'I'm getting you to hospital,' he said, and allowed no argument.

The hospital staff, in a lull between emergencies for once, were friendly but faintly scornful. They took tests, promising the results in twenty-four hours. But really there was not much doubt. It was pretty obvious.

Holly summoned a taxi and drove back to the castle in a daze. She felt stunned.

Jack did not call from Paris. There was nothing unusual in that. But that night, sitting in the garden with all the windows open so she would hear the telephone ring, Holly felt abandoned.

Not that she knew what she would say to him if he did call, she reminded herself. How was she going to put it? There is a possibility that we could have a problem? I know we said this was a marriage of convenience but I'm afraid something inconvenient has come up? No, impossible!

And most impossible of all was the thing that her whole being was screaming at her to tell him: *I need you.*

She slept worse than ever.

The next day brought no test results and no phone call from Jack either. The following morning he called. Holly's heart misgave her. She listened to him talking to the answering machine.

'Hi, Jack here.'

No greeting; no asking after her welfare; certainly no affection. His voice sounded hard. Oh,

God, he must have seen all those lying articles.
Why didn't he *say* so?

'Report over and I'll be back tomorrow. I'm
bringing the office with me—two girls, three guys
will need beds. We've got something to celebrate.'

He rang off. She hugged her arms round herself, suddenly cold.

'Have we?' Holly asked the clicking machine.

The next call gave her the answer.

She went into overdrive. It was a long time
since she had given a party but she remembered
Donna's preparations easily enough. She made a
list and got on the phone.

In the end she decided she needed a boost to
her confidence before she could face Jack's
guests. So she paid her first visit to the hair-
dresser's in five years. It all took much longer
than she'd expected, so when the cab brought her
home she saw cars already in the drive. For a
moment she was shaken by panic.

*I can't face Jack among a lot of strangers. I
just can't.*

But she had no choice. She shot into the house
and did her best to brace herself.

There was a long tiger-striped muslin shirt with
a matching bikini in the wardrobe. The ensemble
had cost so much that it hurt her even to think

about it. It had been a desperation buy at a show mounted by the amazingly expensive local boutique in support of a village charity. Her hostess had made it clear that Mrs Jack Armour was not going to get away without a handsome contribution to funds and Holly, who had not had a swimsuit for five years, had bought the only thing she thought she needed.

Now, looking at herself in the mirror, she wondered if it had been a mistake. Oh, it was gorgeous, all right. Sophisticated and sexy and gorgeous.

And I'm not, thought Holly.

But it was the only thing she had to swim in. And maybe it was camouflage she needed. So she squared her shoulders and went out into the garden to join the party.

Jack must have brought bottles of drink down with him after he'd asked all the guests. There was normally little alcohol in the house. Now, however, there was a tray of glasses and bottles on the wooden table under the willow. Armour Disaster Recovery were sitting by the poolside with fluorescent cocktails in their hands, watching for the arrival of the mystery woman.

Holly made it a good one.

She came out onto the terrace, sunhat in hand, huge sunglasses covering her eyes, and posed against the ivy-covered wall. Just long enough to get their attention. Then she waved and ran lightly down the steps. Whatever her reservations about the outfit's sexiness, it made her look good, she knew.

She went straight to Jack.

He looked down at her. There was not a vestige of feeling in his face. She thought: *He's read those articles.*

'Hi, darling.' When she was nervous her voice went husky. It must have sounded to them all like the last word in sexy intimacy.

She stood on tiptoes and kissed him slowly on the mouth. It was quite deliberate. He could not turn away from her if he wanted all his friends to think they were the ideal couple, after all.

Jack's mouth moved under hers, once. Just a fraction, but it moved. Then he lifted his head and looked down at her. Chilled to the bone, Holly thought: *Read them and believed every word.*

As always, she could not read his expression for certain. But the others had no fault to find. At least one member of the party—a woman—sighed enviously.

Well, thank God for that, thought Holly. She turned to them, hands spread eloquently.

'Hi, everybody. Glad to see you could get away from the office on this beautiful day. The prospect of a swim just too good to resist?'

'You can say that again.' That was patronising Louise. Pretty, patronising Louise.

Holly tensed. 'Well, it's good to see you all,' she said lightly. 'I have a conscience about being the only one using the pool on a day like this.'

She sat down on the moss-covered bank that bordered one side of the pool and looked covertly at Louise. Was she the reason that Jack had brought the whole team down? He always spoke of her with fondness and Holly knew how much he respected her work. She did not think Louise was a replacement for Susana, but she was attractive and her sophistication went deeper than tiger swimwear.

Holly looked at Jack, grateful for the masking sunglasses. It was surprising how deep jealousy could stab, even in a relationship like theirs.

He mixed a bright green cocktail and gave it to her. His lips were smiling. But the smile did not reach his dark eyes. It never did when he looked at her these days. It had not since Ignaz. That stabbed too.

But he was offering an explanation of his unexpected behaviour. *Concentrate,* Holly told herself.

'Spontaneous celebration,' Jack said in his deep voice. 'We got the EU contract.'

Holly was not going to admit she did not know what the EU contract was about. Whatever it was, it had the others all beaming. She raised her glass to them in a toast.

'Congratulations.'

'Yes, it's a real feather in Jack's cap,' said Louise, looking at the tall man with admiration.

And why not? thought Holly, curbing another uncivilised spasm of jealousy. He was the woman's boss. He was successful and generous to his staff. And they had just won an important contract. Besides which, as a man he was a fireball. No one knew that better than Holly. It was no wonder if pretty Louise looked at him as if he were the god Apollo come down to earth.

What was more, Holly reminded herself, that was Jack's business and Jack's alone. By the terms of their agreement Holly had no right to object or even to comment on what he did in his private life. She thought Jack would have forbidden her to be hurt by it as well if it had ever occurred to him that she could be hurt.

These days, of course, they were both of them pretending that she was immune to anything he did. Sometimes Holly had even believed it. Until today, and the news that had made her face the truth she had known in her bones all along.

She was in love with him. More, she thought she had been in love with him from the first moment in Paris. Even their duelling had been a sort of intimacy. She loved him! And she wanted him to love her. Which was hopeless when he loved a shadow from his past. How did a real woman fight the allure of a shadow?

It was terrible to feel so distraught and have to maintain a bright social face. She tried to be interested in the conversation.

'It was Jack who convinced Commissioner Durango,' chimed in one of the men. 'I set out the technical specs but it took Jack's sweet talk to convince them.'

'Well, congratulations to Jack,' said Holly, raising her glass to him too.

She did not mean to sound waspish but that was the way it came out. She saw the others look uncomfortable and could have kicked herself.

But Jack had it in hand. 'Don't worry, darling,' he said lightly. 'Discussion of boring work ends here.'

Holly picked up the hint with the horrible ease. If you lived a lie you got used to covering up the holes.

'Great,' she said gaily. 'What are you doing to celebrate?'

Jack looked at her. 'We thought we'd party,' he said with deliberation. 'Here.'

And he let his eyes drift over her as if they partied together every day—and fell into mutual and voluptuous coupling every night afterwards. A faint colour rose under Holly's tan. Oh, yes, Jack was good at lying too. Except that it was not—wholly—a lie.

For half a heartbeat there was a silence that seemed to slice through Holly's nerves to the wincing core of her. Then she recovered. Living a lie gave you a quick recovery time.

'Wonderful. I *love* spur-of-the-moment parties.'

It was not true. Any more than it was true that he wanted to make love to her or that this was a real marriage.

But they believed it. They expected no less. It went with the wild child reputation Brendan had given her and that, she was beginning to fear, Jack had come to accept.

'I told them you'd enjoy it.' His voice was warm, lazily amused, indulgent. Only his eyes were blank.

She stretched out long tanned legs in front of her and pretended to sip her cocktail.

'Great. Why don't we swim first and then barbecue?' She had borrowed one from the doctor's
wife. 'Then dance out here as long as it stays
warm.' The sound system came from the pub
landlord, whose son had spent a happy couple of
hours rigging it up and selecting CDs to make the
place jump. So much friendly support had to be
repaid. 'I've asked a few neighbours to join us.'

'I knew I could leave it to you,' Jack said idly.
'You're the party expert.'

Holly's heart sank. She did not let it show.

'Fortunately it's the night for it. Have you all
brought something to swim in?'

'Not like yours,' said Louise ruefully.

Holly looked down. So the tiger stripes were
doing the business, Holly thought cynically. Or
maybe it was the long tanned legs, the soft cloud
of hair streaked to an artistic and expensive
tawny, or the suite of gold chains she wore on
her wrist.

Whatever it was, they were looking. And ad-
miring. Envying, even—at least, some of the
women were. Which was what she wanted. It
meant that they were seeing what they expected
to see: Jack Armour's indulged and wayward
wife, not a woman on the edge of despair.

She said now, 'Well, the water is warm. Swim when you want. There are towels in the downstairs bathroom.'

She stood up.

'Don't rush off. You haven't finished your drink,' said Jack.

He watched her narrowly. Holly felt horribly self-conscious.

To hide it she pulled a laughing face. 'I'm sorry, darling. This is absolutely filthy. What is it? Toothpaste and advocaat?'

A couple of the group looked uncomfortable. Jack was unmoved.

'I shouldn't expect you to drink anything but champagne,' he said smoothly.

So he *had* believed the articles. How could he, when he had seen with his own eyes the garret she'd lived in?

'I'll come in with you and make sure it's properly chilled.'

He slid his arm round her waist and strolled her back into the house.

The muslin was no barrier to the heat of his body. His arm felt like an iron bar straight out of the furnace. The sensation was so strong, Holly could barely speak.

I'm carrying his child. He has his arm round me. And we're like strangers.

Once they were out of sight of the pool party, inside the house, she removed herself from his grip. He did not resist. But he did look at her with that intent, considering look.

'Have you got anything you want to tell me?'

Holly went very still.

'Such as?'

'Maybe a full confession,' he said. He sounded amused but she knew him well enough to hear the anger licking through.

She began to tremble. 'What sort of confession?'

'Well, I'd rather have heard about your adolescent rebellions from you than the morning newspapers,' he said, suddenly savage.

She began to feel sick again. *Oh, very convenient, Holly.*

'We can't talk about this now.'

'When can we talk about it?'

Holly's sense of fair play was offended. 'When *your* guests have gone.'

'Oh, no, we'll talk before then.' He showed his teeth in an unamused smile. 'We'll talk tonight.'

She did not know how she got through the party, though everyone else had a great time. The village guests brought drink and all the women came bearing food of some sort.

Holly was grateful. Rushing about among her guests, she managed to avoid coming face to face with Jack.

Until the end of the evening, of course. Someone had changed the music and the guests were slow dancing dreamily under the stars. Holly had changed into a long cotton skirt and T-shirt by then. But she still shivered.

Warm arms closed round her.

'Dance with me,' said Jack in her ear.

She remembered watching him dance with other women on the beach at their wedding. She unwrapped his arms.

'No.'

He buried his face in her loosened, expensively scented hair. 'Are you telling me you don't want to?' His arms crept round her waist again.

How was it possible to hurt this much and still keep smiling? Holly's face felt as if it had been set with hair spray into an expression of party cheer.

'No, I don't want to dance,' she said steadily. 'You don't trust me and I—don't like you in this mood.'

His arms tightened. 'What mood is that, darling?'

'Cynical.'

With sudden energy, she pushed him away and turned. He looked down at her as if he had never seen her before.

'Cynical or not, I still want you.' His voice was raw. 'Just like you want me.' He reached for her.

Holly could not bear any more. She pushed past him and ran for the house. Tears were spilling down her cheeks.

He let her go. No one else noticed.

She ran to the one place in the house where she thought he would not look for her. The minstrels' gallery was above the main hall, not much more than an extended balcony. But someone had dumped some old furniture up there. She took refuge among decaying damask and wormy pine, huddling down on the floor with her knees under her chin.

The music died. The dancing stopped. She heard the last of the guests go to bed. And still she sat there, tear-stained but dry-eyed now. Jack put out the lights and started to tread heavily up the stairs. Holly held her breath.

The door to the gallery opened.

'Time to talk,' he said, and flicked a switch.

Holly blinked in the sudden glare. The minstrels' gallery was lit by one bulb flickering from a fraying cord. The uncertain shadows made him seem taller and nakedly powerful. Holly caught her breath. The little sound resonated like a scream under the echoing rafters.

'Are you *afraid* of me?' He sounded incredulous.

Holly got painfully to her feet, fighting pins and needles. 'No, of course not.'

She bent over, rubbing her calf muscles.

'Then why the melodrama?'

'Melodrama? Me?' She was furious. It was better than dissolving into weak tears. 'You were the one who couldn't bear to be alone with me so you brought back your whole damned office.'

'Couldn't—' He stopped. 'Is that what you thought?'

She stopped rubbing her muscles, although the pain was excruciating.

'Isn't it true? You saw what those newspapers said about me and you—' But she couldn't go on. The weak tears were victorious after all.

Jack said flatly, 'They had a full-scale celebration prepared in London. They've worked for over a year on this contract. I couldn't get out of it. But I was desperate to get back to you. The only thing I could think of was to bring the revels with me.'

'Oh.'

He heard the doubt in her voice.

'Yes, I've seen the press cuttings. Yes, I want to know how much truth there is in them. But the main reason I'm here is because I didn't want you to be on your own.'

Holly straightened. All she could think was: *He's leaving me.*

'On my own? Why? What's going to happen?'

'I'm afraid Brendan Sugrue has caught up with us. It was only going to be a matter of time, after that damned *Elegance* article.'

'Oh,' said Holly blankly.

Compared with the disaster of Jack leaving, Brendan Sugrue's pursuit seemed suddenly unimportant.

Jack misinterpreted her reaction. 'Don't look like that. My secretary stalled him. We can handle this.'

It was his reassuring voice. He was the calm negotiator, preparing to deal with an opponent. Not her lover protecting her. *I want the lover,* thought Holly rebelliously.

But Jack did not see it.

'I was half afraid he'd get here before I could. You weren't picking up the phone and I didn't want to leave something like that on the machine. He'll be here tomorrow for sure.'

He was so convinced that she would be falling apart that Holly did not know how to react. The days when she had been afraid of Brendan Sugrue seemed a century ago instead of just a few months. Her need to get away from Sugrue and the whole family inheritance seemed negligible compared with the need that gnawed at her now.

She retreated, shrugging. 'Let him come.'

'You're ready to face him?'

She had other, more important concerns now. Her terror of Brendan's bullying seemed childish in retrospect. She was infinitely more afraid of the way Jack Armour could make her feel just by looking at her. Just by coming up behind her and breathing into her hair.

'Why not?'

Somehow she had managed to back herself against the edge of the balustrade. Jack did not move. There was the whole width of the balcony between them. But she could feel the heat of his body, his breath.

She thought: *Hold me.*

The force of her need was so strong it was almost as if she had spoken aloud. With a little moan of shame, she pressed her hands to her cheeks. He had told her in set terms that he did not love her, she was too young for him. Yet here she was virtually throwing herself at him. She could not bear it.

'Go away,' she said in a muffled voice.

Suddenly he was no longer several feet away. The balustrade began to dig into her back. Her world swung wildly as he took her chin in his hand and forced her to meet his eyes.

He said in a low voice, 'Holly we have got to stop tearing at each other like this. You want me. I want you. If that's all we have, then let's build what we can on that.'

Yesterday, it would have been enough. She would have fallen into his arms weeping. But today she knew she was carrying his child. And it had to be love or nothing.

She said, 'I can't.'

And put a hand on the top of her stomach in a protective gesture as old as time.

His eyes flared. Then went utterly blank.

'Don't ask me to—' Her voice gave out.

He could have been turned to marble. She brushed past him and her shoulder felt bruised. He made no move to stop her.

Holly fled.

CHAPTER TEN

HOLLY slept better that night than she had done for weeks but she still woke before dawn. Her eyes drifted open as busy birdsong started in the trees. She was smiling.

I feel happy? Why do I feel so happy?

She stirred; and remembered.

Jack was here. She was carrying his child. And he was *here*.

Then, of course, everything else came back. His shock last night. Had he realised that she was pregnant? At the time she had been certain of it. Certain, too, that he was horrified. Now she was not so sure. Surely he would have said *something*?

Well, they would have to talk about it today, as soon as the guests had gone. Meanwhile there was a party to clear up after. Holly pulled on jeans and a cotton shirt and went to see what needed doing.

She had no experience at all in clearing up after parties. Donna had had servants and, before that, her mother had not had parties. But she had learned a lot in Chef Pierre's kitchen and she enjoyed practical tasks. She loaded the dishwasher in the devastated kitchen and went looking for more debris.

Outside, the dew was still on the grass. It frosted the glasses and bowls that had been left out last night. The air was cool and full of the scents of grasses, sharp as champagne at the back of her throat. Blackbirds trilled. And last night Jack had held her and said he wanted her.

Holly gave a sigh of something between pain and delight. Wanting was not enough. It would never be enough. But she suspected it was more than many people had. Maybe he was right, after all, and they could build something on that fragile foundation. Their baby deserved—

Her thoughts skittered to a halt. No, she wanted Jack to stay with her because he loved her. Not because he was a responsible man who had fathered an unlooked-for child. Her baby would be loved, whatever happened. But if Jack stayed with her it had to be because she, not Susana Montijo, was the love of his life.

Fat chance, thought Holly, wincing.

She attacked the clearing up with fury. By the time Jack came down, the kitchen was sparkling. A row of dishes to be returned to their owners was set out in the dining room. And Holly was filled with a grim satisfaction.

By contrast, Jack looked rough. He had not shaved and his eyes were wild. He looked at her narrowly.

'You all right?'

'I'm fine.' She was desperate to talk to him; tell him about the baby. But she could not, not with all these people in the house.

He seemed ill at ease. 'You shouldn't have done all that alone. I would have helped.'

She put on some coffee.

'I like getting things back into order,' she said with constraint.

'Evidently,' he said drily. He pushed a hand through his hair. 'What a crazy weekend to have people to stay. Look, I'll get rid of them. Send them off sightseeing to Ludlow or something. We need to talk.'

'I know.'

No matter what happened she loved him, she reminded herself. She would treasure it always, wherever she went. And she would have his child to treasure too.

Jack banged a fist into the wall. *'Damn!'*

The house guests were surprisingly accommodating. They took maps and guidebooks and piled into their cars with alacrity. It was the party guests who were the problem. All through the morning there was a steady stream of people dropping by to say thank you and pick up their crockery. The dining room emptied of glass and china and filled up instead with garden produce and bouquets. It was a long time since there had been a party at the castle.

'We must do it again,' said Jack, between frustration and despairing amusement, as they saw off yet another grateful party goer.

That got through Holly's unnatural calm. His laughing remark implied a shared future that they both knew was impossible. Or did it? She turned away.

'Holly?'

The phone was ringing. She went towards it. Jack stopped her with a word.

'I love you,' he said quietly.

She halted as if he had tapped her with a magician's wand. Her mind reeled.

She did not turn. Jack did not touch her.

'I can't take any more of this.' His voice was low but very level. 'If you don't care for me, I can accept that. But I can't go on pretending.'

Holly could not believe it. She was shaken to the heart. She began to tremble.

'Jack—'

But there was no time. The ring of the phone was insistent. And yet another car was coming up the drive.

'This will be the Ransomes,' she said distract-edly. 'I'll get their salad bowl if you answer that.'

'And then—'

She looked at him then. She hardly recognised him: the intentness, the tenderness, the unmistak-eable sincerity.

He touched her cheek briefly.

Holly was dazed. Disbelieving. But that sincerity made him vulnerable suddenly. It demanded an answer.

'Yes,' she said.

He went and so did she. But when she came out again, with the wooden bowl in her hands, it was not the Ransomes. The man getting out of the driver's seat was a tall commanding figure she had been afraid of all her adult life. But Jack loved her. She looked at him with absolute indifference.

'Hello, Brendan.'

Someone else emerged from the passenger's seat. Holly's eyebrows rose.

'And Homer. What a surprise,' she said faintly.

Brendan slammed the car door and swaggered over to her. Why had she never noticed that ostentatious gait before? she thought, despising herself. He behaved like a bully in a school playground. If you weren't afraid of him, he was nothing.

'OK Holly. What mess have you got yourself into now?'

That was Brendan all over. No pretence at friendliness and straight into the middle of an argument that you had finished weeks ago in another country. Suddenly, gloriously, Holly wanted to laugh.

'No mess,' she said gravely. 'But you can congratulate me on my marriage if you like.'

He loomed over her menacingly.

'Marriage? That's what that lawyer said! So where's the fond husband?'

She stood her ground. She even smiled.

'Inside, taking a phone call.'

That disconcerted him. He exchanged a look with Homer.

The shorter man came forward. He hadn't changed either, Holly saw. Still pale and blank-eyed.

Homer said, 'Holly, my dear child, this can't go on. You must realise you are a very rich young woman.'

'Yes, I realise that,' Holly said drily. She put the bowl down upon the ground and folded her arms. 'So?'

'Well, how long have you known this man you say you want to marry?'

'Have married,' she corrected quietly.

Brendan burst in. 'Doesn't sound like a legal ceremony to me. We're checking.'

Homer brushed that aside. 'How long?'

'Since April,' Holly admitted.

'A few months. Exactly. So what do you really know about him?'

'I—'

'He's an adventurer. Never stays in one place for two minutes together. No real substance to him. And his company needs money, did you know that?'

Holly surveyed him for a long, level minute.

'Clever,' she said at last. 'I always knew there had to be some reason why Brendan brought you in to run the company. Now I see what it is. You're a real snake, aren't you, Homer?'

He did not lose his smile. 'If you mean I'm a businessman who recognises the way other businessmen think, then, yes, I'm a snake.'

There was a small sound behind her. She turned and saw Jack standing in the doorway. He looked appalled.

Holly could not bear it. She went to him and put her hand in his without even thinking about it.

'He hasn't asked me for money and I haven't offered him any. But I will.'

Jack was taken aback. 'Holly—'

She ignored him. 'It will be an inheritance for our child.'

Jack jumped as if she had put an electric shock through him. His fingers clenched convulsively round hers.

Brendan gave a roar. 'You mean you—'

Holly smiled. 'You can congratulate us, Brendan.'

'Darling,' said Jack, and pulled her roughly back into his arms. She could feel his heart hammering against her shoulder blade.

Homer, horribly, was still smiling. 'Even more reason to take you back with us. You must see that as a concerned guardian Brendan really can't allow you to stay with a man who seduced you and made you go through some dubious marriage ceremony. Especially when you've known him for so little time.'

Brendan took his cue after only the slightest hesitation. 'Absolutely. I'll get the lawyers on to it right away.'

Jack looked down at her. Whatever he saw in her face made his arm go round her, clamping her to him as if they were going to climb a dangerous path side by side.

'Brendan doesn't get a vote,' he told her calmly. He looked up and his eyes clashed with

Homer's. 'Nor, for that matter, do you. On your way, gentlemen.'

Brendan began to shout with incoherent fury but the only reaction that Homer gave was a slight narrowing of the eyes.

'How much to stay away from her?' he said softly.

Holly thought Jack was going to hit him. She held her breath. Her hand twisted in his in silent protest.

Jack raised their cupped hands to his mouth and kissed her knuckles reassuringly. He looked over the top of her hand at Homer. He laughed.

That did get a reaction. Homer's face darkened.

'Oh, you've got yourself a real thing there, haven't you?' he jeered.

Jack looked down at Holly. 'Yes,' he said softly. 'Yes, I think I have.'

Her eyes flew to his. She thought she had never seen such warmth in them. Or such pride.

'Jack?' she said uncertain, wondering, hoping against hope.

Brendan shouted, 'Undue influence. The kid was so crazy she'd run off with anyone. Hell, she *did*. I'll have it annulled.'

Jack hardly looked at him. His eyes were too busy scanning Holly's softly flushed face. 'Too late,' he said with immense satisfaction.

Holly's colour deepened. But she bit back a smile and had to look away.

He turned his head to survey the men briefly. 'Make your mind up, Sugrue. Either it's real or it isn't. If it isn't, there can't have been undue influence. If it is, you can't get an annulment.' He looked back at Holly and kissed her hand again. 'Quite apart from what Holly wants.'

All Brendan's spurious concern for her evaporated in a blast of pure fury.

'Holly wants a good time. Any guy will do,' he spat.

Holly cried, 'It's not true—'

But Jack was before her. He dropped the arm round her waist and put her behind him.

'Yes, you've said that before,' he said, in his quiet negotiating tone. 'She's my wife. I know which of you I believe.'

But Brendan was feeling too vicious to be wise.

'She's wild—irresponsible—*anybody's*...'

Jack hit him. Self-controlled, diplomatic, problem-solving Jack thudded one angry blow into that bull-like body. Brendan fell to the ground.

Holly grabbed Jack. He would hate that loss of control, she thought. His arm went round her, tight as a vice. She could feel the tremors in his muscles and knew how little it would take for him to fight Brendan in earnest.

Brendan seemed to see it too, at last. He sprawled on the ground, glaring up at Jack nearly incoherent. He switched his gaze to Holly.

'You think you know this guy?' He was winded and spluttering with rage. 'You don't. False pretences…'

It was time, thought Holly, to fight her own battle. And finish it once and for all. She looked down at him levelly.

'Yes, I know Jack's company needs money. I knew that before I even realised I would have any. When the lawyer told me—' she hesitated, then gave a small shrug '—well, that's why I came to live here in his house. I couldn't do much for him but I thought I might be able to do that, at least. It's nothing compared with what he's given me.'

Jack's eyes left Brendan, and flew to her face. The adrenaline-fuelled trembling stopped as if a machine had switched itself off. The arm round her waist became painful.

'Go away,' Jack said. He was himself again, in control and knowing exactly what he wanted. He gazed deep into Holly's eyes. 'Go away, *now*.'

Brendan scrambled to his feet, mouthing threats. But Homer knew when he was beaten. He drew his cousin away, still fuming. Jack and Holly hardly noticed them go.

Jack said, 'I want to make love to you.'

'Yes.'

'I love you. I want you to know that.'

Holly leaned against him. 'Yes.'

'Now?' he said into her hair, urgent, uncharacteristically uncertain. 'Please. I need to show you—'

'Yes,' said Holly.

Later they lay in each other's arms in the four-poster. Jack stroked her hair.

'Oh, God, you are wonderful and I am so lucky.'

She breathed in his scent, her fingers curling with pleasure. 'Mmm.'

'I love you. If you'd asked me at Easter, I'd have said I'd never say that again.'

Holly kissed his shoulder. 'Susana?'

'Yes. I was crazy about her.' He was shaken by a little laugh. 'In fact I've realised these last few weeks that's exactly what it was. Crazy.'

'Why?'

'Oh, who knows? The time was right, I suppose.'

She raised herself onto her elbows. 'Tell?'

He caressed the curve of her eyebrow. 'She surprised me—how much she meant to me. I'd

had my fun but I was always rather cold-blooded.
With women, I mean.'

Holly suppressed a chuckle. He flicked her
nose.

'Sexpot,' he said peacefully.

She wriggled with appreciation. 'All your doing. Tell me about Susana.'

'She was a translator who worked with me. It
was a terrible time: revolution and earthquake si-
multaneously. When I knew her she was legally
separated because her husband beat her up. He
was in hiding and she was responsible for her
younger brothers and sister and half of his family
as well. I wanted to take care of her. We had a
weekend in the hills.'

Holly stared down at him, her smile dying.
'One weekend? That's all?'

'Yes.'

'And on the basis of that you decided she was
the love of your life?'

She was horrified. How could she compete with
an attraction like that? All her insecurities, which
his lovemaking had banished, came back to flay
her.

Jack cupped her cheek. 'I hadn't met you then.
I didn't know what it could be like,' he said soberly.

But Holly was too shaken to be reassured. He sat up, carrying her with him, and propped her possessively against his chest.

'Holly, listen, my love. You don't know what I was like. My parents were good people but they shouldn't have had children. We didn't kiss in our house; we saluted. Susana *felt* so much; and what she felt she talked about. It was a fairy-tale, a fantasy. I thought I could take care of her and of course I couldn't. That's why it ended. Because she would not leave all the people she loved and I couldn't see why.' He brushed his cheek against her hair. 'Do you understand?'

'So she broke your heart?'

He grimaced. 'That's a very female way of looking at it.'

'I am female,' said Holly, her confidence returning. 'You were still carrying a torch for her when we met.'

'No,' he said slowly. 'Not really. It was all so long ago. What still hurt was the fact that I hadn't been able to rescue her.'

'So I was your second attempt at the damsel in distress?'

'Maybe a little.' His arms tightened. 'You were so afraid of Sugrue. Nobody should be that afraid.'

'I was very young and he's a bully,' Holly excused herself. 'But the person who really scared me was Homer. He seemed to have no feelings. Nothing I could say made any difference.'

'I've seen dead fish with more expression,' agreed Jack.

'Until this morning. You scared him,' said Holly with satisfaction.

Jack was startled. 'I—er—got carried away there,' he admitted. 'I know you don't like violence. But when Sugrue said that, I just saw red. Sorry.'

Holly turned her face against his chest. Her voice was muffled. 'Didn't you believe him? Not a bit?'

'No.'

'But—'

'I've lived with you. I've worked with you. I've made love with you,' he said quietly. 'Whatever you do, you do from the heart.'

'Oh.' She breathed in his scent as if it were the life force. 'Not wild? Not—' she forced herself to say it '—*anybody's*?'

He was forceful. 'Never. You were too self-contained, if anything. It took me for ever to get you to let me in,' he added ruefully.

She looked up, startled by the look on his face. 'I was afraid,' she said excusingly.

'Not afraid any more?'

Holly kissed him. 'No. Got myself pretty straight now, with your help. Consider me rescued.'

But he did not laugh. 'You were so *young*. There were a couple of times I thought you were afraid of me, too.'

Holly shook her head slowly. 'Not you. How you felt, maybe.' She had a sudden, vivid vision of that surging frustration, that inflammable mixture below the cool surface, that she had sensed in him that day in the grubby room in Montmartre. 'How you made me feel.'

'And now?'

She moved against him with deliberate provocation. 'What does it feel like?'

'Heaven,' said Jack, taking her back under the sheet with him. 'Absolute heaven.'

EPILOGUE

THE group of international journalists was in an exceptionally mellow mood. The conference speakers had been brief, the stories dramatic and the Sugar Island venue unusually exotic. Now Armour Disaster Recovery was hosting a champagne reception complete with steel band.

'Great stuff,' said an English foreign correspondent.

'Great company,' said a German financial journalist. 'That new capital last year has really made them a force to be reckoned with.'

'Great family,' said American Rita Caruso, pointing her camera.

The object of her attention waved to her. Jack Armour was commanding in a tuxedo while Holly looked delectable in Caribbean print. Her golden-brown hair was swept up for the occasion and she was wearing the long diamond drops that Jack had given her when the third member of the group was born.

'Oh, you're too young for this,' Jack had said, torn between a new father's pride and unexpected remorse.

'Anyone would be too young for that baby,' retorted Holly, startled by the new arrival's competence.

Now Anthony Francis Armour, known as Einstein, waved fat arms in the direction of a passing champagne flute.

'No,' said Jack, steering the waiter out of his son's range. He relieved Holly of the wriggling burden. 'Want to talk to Caruso?'

She shook her head. 'She's a nice woman. But I thought you would never forgive me when she wrote that article calling you romantic.'

Jack's eyes glinted down at her over his son's dark head.

'Are you saying I'm not romantic?'

Holly glinted a laugh back up at him. 'Heaven forbid.'

'Or that I should be ashamed of it?'

'Never.'

'So why don't you want to talk to Caruso?'

'Pure jealousy,' said Holly with calm. She nodded to Paula Vincent, who was showing a suffering Ramon several hundred photographs of the midnight wedding. 'She thinks you're a hunk.'

Jack's eyes lit with that private laughter that turned her bones to water even now. 'So I am,' he said outrageously. 'Your hunk. What's your problem?'

Holly dropped her head against his shoulder. 'No problem.'

He bent his head. 'Happy?' he said in a voice that was meant only for her.

'Mmm.'

'Can I do anything to make you happier?'

Holly was seized by a naughty impulse. 'We-ell...'

Jack raised a wicked eyebrow.

'We got married on that beach. But we never—'

He laughed aloud. 'You want to make love on a Caribbean beach? A respectable wife and mother like you?'

Holly sighed. 'I suppose it's a silly idea.'

He raised an imperious finger. Paula Vincent detached herself from Ramon, to his great relief.

'It's a wonderful idea,' Jack said calmly. 'Which is why Paula has added a full baby-sitting service to her range.'

Holly's conscience was uneasy. 'But Einstein doesn't know her.'

'Einstein likes to party,' said Jack unanswerably, as his son stuck an exploratory finger in someone's rum punch and sucked it thoughtfully. He transferred the baby to Paula. 'That's my boy. See you for breakfast, Paula. Come on, honey, let me take you away from all this.'

Paula sighed romantically and waved them off.

'You,' said Holly in the beach-buggy beside him, her hair blowing free from its pins, 'are a tyrant.'

'Because I arranged for you to do what you want to do?'

'Before I said I wanted it.'

'That just makes me a sensitive and empathic individual,' said Jack with odious complacency.

Holly laughed but it was breathless.

'Besides, I want it, too.'

She gave a pleasurable little shiver. 'Do you?'

'Until I met you, I would have stayed at that party and networked. Probably made a couple of contacts, then gone home and written up think pieces for their breakfast mail. Thanks to you, I'm now the sort of man who kidnaps respectable women and carries them off to empty beaches to ravish them.'

'Wow. Is that what you're going to do?'

'Right now,' said Jack, his voice uneven in spite of the laughter, 'all I can think of is taking your hair down and your clothes off and making love to you until you scream loud enough to frighten the fish.'

Holly looked at him in the shadows. He was her husband, her sparring partner, her friend and the father of her child. And her lover.

'Yes, *please*,' she said.